# WHY
# MYSTERY
# MATTERS

By

NEIL NIXON & E.K. KNIGHT

Olcan Press

First published by Olcan Press on 15th April 2023

Olcan Print/Press are a subsidiary of the Olcan Group

6 Park Hill, Ealing
London, W5 2JN, UK
Email: team@olcan.co
www.olcan.co

Content copyright © Neil Nixon

For permission contact:
team@olcan.co

A CIP record of this publication is available from the British Library.

First printed April 2023
Paperback ISBN: 978-1-7391440-4-3

# Contents

# The Authors

 **Neil Nixon** has been writing for publication since he was a student, a working life that has taken in 30 books authored or edited and contributions to around two dozen other titles. His scripting is diverse enough to have earned a Sony Academy Award nomination for Best Single Radio Drama and include work for the glove puppet Sooty, who typically doesn't speak. Neil has also produced journalism, comedy, and work for the stage. After a lengthy academic career, a significant part of which involved founding and running the UK's first higher education course in Professional Writing he now combines work in corporate PR with writing and live speaking. Neil met his partner in this project when she applied for the Professional Writing course. Neil has the website neilnixon.com.

 **E K Knight** produced this book "with" Neil. At one point E K's words take over a chapter end completely, elsewhere the planning and shaping of the whole project involved two-way communication and one lengthy fireside meeting. E K Knight lives in a world of dark fantasy, revels in the details and writes down enough of what transpires to be sitting on the basis of an estimable cult success. By contrast, E K's visits to the more mundane realms we all share are less vivid and exciting, though book selling has its moments!

# INTRODUCTION

This is a book about mystery, not a book about famous mysteries – though some of them will be mentioned and explored. The book is about mystery itself; what it is, how we experience it and – most importantly – why we should celebrate it and realise its value in all our lives. I'm not here to focus on any one mystery or one person's experience of the mysterious, so this book is not promoting any philosophical or religious view of mystery. We will – however- investigate experiences that matter in philosophy and religion. The point of this book is simply to isolate mystery, consider it for what it is and what it means and focus on the value we get from mystery – in whatever form we encounter it. Some of the examples presented will be those most often mentioned when mysteries are debated. So personal experiences of a god and the complicated questions of what might explain UFO sightings will both feature in our journey. Elsewhere, I make no apologies for bringing in the most mundane and everyday examples of the mysterious. Those examples are here to demonstrate that mystery is part of who we are and what we do; a part we sometimes fail to value as much as we should. Similarly, I make no apologies for presenting a short investigation.

This is the literary equivalent of a talk to a group. I want to share some knowledge and insights and leave you with the information and the ideas you will require to explore the subject in more depth. Your exploration could take the form of the classic - search online, read and talk to others -development of ideas. It could also take the form of an inward journey. Most likely, it will involve inward and outward travel. All of which is very appropriate because one of the most enduring mysteries for all of us involves trying to work out who we are, where we are going (or if, indeed, we are going anywhere), and whether any of it has a profound meaning. As a rule, answering those questions for yourself involves some outside checking of information and realities but all of that only makes sense when answers feel right to you, personally. The point of this book is not to present easy answers, though – hopefully – it presents easy guidance to the places where those answers are most likely to be found.

# CHAPTER ONE

# WHAT IS MYSTERY?

Defining mystery is not easy. Though it is simple enough to quote a dictionary definition. The first Google hit presenting itself as this chapter started was – predictably – from dictionary.com which identified mystery as "anything that is kept secret or remains unexplained or unknown." This was the first of six definitions on the same page; the others being definitions that make sense in context. So "mystery" also refers to a particular kind of literary text, the type of experience that only makes sense in the light of some divine revelation or the kind of affair or event that can't easily be explained. Two things are clear from this array of explanations. Firstly, mystery exists because we experience the mysterious. We have feelings, hunches about things and responses in our reasoning that attempt to make sense of what we fail to understand. Things remain secret or unknown to us. Many of the things we find mysterious continue existing whether we notice, or not. For example, the South African museum curator Marjorie Courtenay-Latimer was so fascinated by a particular fish collected within the catch of a local angler on 23 December 1938 that she contacted a noted ichthyologist (expert in the history, science, and behaviour of fish). The investigation that followed confirmed the fish as a Coelacanth; a creature known to science but believed extinct for around 65 million years. Much at that point was mysterious. How had this fish survived when most of its closest relatives were clearly extinct, how had the fish managed to avoid presenting itself on the fossil record for so long and did this discovery suggest more Coelacanths remained to be found? As the field of Ichthyology reacted to one of the most intriguing discoveries of the 20th century these questions formed the basics for the investigations that followed, which led – amongst other things – to the discovery of another species of Coelacanth which lives in the oceans off Indonesia. The mysteries of how and why this fish had survived for so long have yielded some truths and more mystery, which is generally the case when science investigates a strange phenomenon. However, with regards to mystery itself and the purpose of this book the Coelacanth shows us something completely different to the conundrums it presents to science. It demonstrates quite clearly that a lot of what we experience as mystery is our own creation. Coelacanths survived off the scientific record for 65 million years without spending time worrying about how the world was changing or what they should do about it. As fish they exist mainly to feed and reproduce. They did therefore react to changes in their environment, enduring against our expectations. They didn't think reflectively about any of this, they simply went about surviving, until we discovered them, having previously listed them as extinct.

As humans we choose to investigate, learn and exist for a number of purposes. We have learned to value the unexplained and unknown as the starting point for our own learning, and the reappearance of a species thought extinct was therefore a celebrated mystery in 1938. But we make our own mysteries because we decide what matters and how we will engage with our mysteries.

Mystery may have meanings as a word, but for most of us the thing that really matters is how we apply those meanings to our own lives and how we experience mystery. If we consider the definitions presented from the dictionary quoted above, we can see that, in some forms, mystery is quite literally a commodity. In other words, something that can be bought, sold, or traded. If the commodity in question is a detective novel and the genre written on the back is "mystery" then this is clearly true. Bookshops and online retailers will happily present these stories in one area knowing that a willing audience will part with money to own them. Some of the more spiritual sides of mystery do not lend themselves so easily to such commodification. But they do become commodified when the stories of those who have experienced mystery are turned into product. In some cases, the fact the events themselves are mysterious becomes the basis of a small industry producing products. The reported miraculous visions of the Virgin Mary in 1917 at Fatima in Portugal by three girls who were all daughters of local farming families includes a tale of the truly miraculous. Known as "The Miracle of the Sun" the claim is that in front of a crowd of somewhere between 30,000 and 100,000 people the Sun emerged from rainclouds duller than usual, radiating different colours of light and — according to some eyewitnesses – dived towards the Earth before regaining its usual place in the sky.

*Witnesses to the Miracle of the Sun*

Around the same time witnesses reported rain-soaked clothing becoming instantly dry and the same sudden drying occurring to the wet ground on which people stood. Predictably, there are counter claims suggesting all the elements of this miracle were simply misperceptions. The one photograph taken at the event showing the Sun doesn't display anything particularly strange. The sightings of Our Lady of Fatima with the attendant Miracle of the Sun remain mysterious and the need for people to know continues to drive an industry including publications and visits to the site of the events. Some people continue to report personal experiences related to the mysterious sightings. On the centenary of one of the main events, 13 May 2017, two of the three children who experienced the visions were canonized. Some Catholics now pray to them and may experience these recently created saints intervening in their lives as a result of these prayers. All of the above doesn't prove the reality of what happened in 1917 one way or the other. In fact, the ongoing activities to prove and disprove the claims ensure that accepting the events as a genuine religious miracle is only ever likely to be a matter of faith. These paranormal claims, along with countless others involving everything from alien abduction to the ability to heal others via prayer do – however – show us the power of mystery to grip the human imagination. They also demonstrate that we value individuals who have had direct contact with something truly mysterious.

Even the pragmatically minded among us still value mystery in its most mundane forms. Perhaps the simplest demonstration of this in most lives comes in those moments when we are challenged with answering a difficult question before producing the perfect answer and then asking ourselves where, exactly, that sudden insight came from.

Mystery is also central to our growth as individuals. It contributes to this growth in many ways. One of the most obvious involves the way mystery is built into our education. One specific example is a formal requirement for all educators in the UK and was part of my working life for two decades. All of Britain's nationally recognized educational programs are subject to a benchmarking process whereby they are obliged to prove that the activities they provide for students are of a suitable standard for the level of education involved. There is no benchmarking guideline or statement that requires "learners must understand mystery" but there are many places in which creating mystery and obliging learners to manage their way to clarity is essential. I developed and ran the UK's first higher education course in Professional Writing and in the second year of that program we were faced with a benchmarking obligation to show that students were learning to work within the limitations of their own knowledge. Taken literally this seems nonsensical because it obliges those halfway through their degree studies to limit the knowledge base they use to contribute to the work they hand in. In fact, it's a vital check on academic progress and essential preparation for the

7

challenges to come. What it means in practice is that students are guided through work in which there is less reward than they received the previous year available for them producing factual arguments, and more reward available when they demonstrate levels of self-knowledge and astute judgement in solving problems. A practical example on the course I ran involved a couple of assignments we called Put up or Shut up 1 & 2. Put up...1 obliged our students to locate the details of one specific job they could do having graduated and the second Put up...assignment obliged them to find some target to whom they could submit a specific creative idea. The self-knowledge assessed in both cases revolved around the decision making of individual students and how they could evidence their own qualities and reasoning as they made these decisions. The reality check to stop this whole exercise becoming a collision of naval gazing and wishful thinking was provided by the obligation for the individuals to measure all their arguments against a job spec they brought along and discussed in class, and against submission guidelines available to the public on places like the websites of magazines or literary agents. On the surface the assignment worked well and usually proved we had no best or worst students because everyone identified a particular target, one unlikely to appeal to anyone else in their class. The all-important element of mystery in the process came in those moments when students felt some personal urge or hunch about the right decision. They recognized that there was no right answer in a traditional sense, only an answer they could best argue was right for them. Crudely, the one that felt right. On those occasions that class presentations or the handed in assignments gave us insights into the unique qualities of the individuals there were often moments when they would ask themselves, and us; "where did that come from?"

A prosaic answer to that question would start with some consideration of the work done by various areas of the brain and consider the neural pathways we all develop. These allow us to store and access information, mixing thoughts and personal experience to help us manage our lives. Doing this allows us to present a revelatory and reflective thought in a few well-chosen words. What matters in those moments, and what matters repeatedly to human beings who experience similar moments in hugely varied circumstances is that brief experience of mystery. That feeling of being ambushed by the uncanny and knowing with complete certainty it came from you. In the assignment example quoted above, I might have designed an academic tool that

9

made this process more likely to occur but all I really did – apart from advancing individuals two assignments closer to completing their second years – was to arrange the circumstances so that some minor revelations would regularly occur in class, and then reward these results in a way that aimed to make the revelations contagious for the whole group.

None of this was new and examined over human history the use of mystery to develop insight and a fleeting experience of the uncanny has been the bedrock of some academic enquiry. Dialectic, or dialectical method collides two opposing views with the intention that each demolishes the other's argument until all that remains is the closest it is possible to get to the truth. This definition is an oversimplification of a process that goes back to the Greeks. Modifications and varying applications include Medieval and Marxist models. The process generally eschews any emotional or subjective elements but – ironically - the experience of engaging in a dialectical argument is often emotional and taxing to the point it feels like your individual personality, sometimes your very essence, is under challenge. This is certainly the case if the subject under debate involves rationalizing your life choices. Those studying religion have their own traditions of dialectic, notably some followers of the Bahá'í faith who see a mutual dependence between science and religion and regard the ideal state of affairs as being a complete harmony of the two. The Bahá'í faith teaches that God is essentially unknowable, and we come closest to an understanding through the examples presented by the greatest prophets. A secular interpretation of this view sees it as the notion that we are guided through the experience of dialectic, and mysterious and uncanny truths can be revealed. Either way, there's a strong suggestion that reducing all insights to concentrating on facts and traditional learning limits our understanding of who we are. Ultimately, dialectic in its academic form is a demanding process that draws on all the resources a human can muster. In the most widely used model of scholarship dialectic is the basis of peer review; the process within which academic advancement is achieved when new discoveries in all disciplines are written up and presented for publication. At which point, others are given the chance to review and challenge the discoveries. Reviewed in this way by academic peers the process of challenge, argument and advancement is intended to work to the benefit of human knowledge. In practice it is far from perfect, but it does frequently revolve around items of mystery. These mysteries include everything from nature behaving in ways we don't understand to those moments when humans do the unexpected. If researchers can record and describe the mysteries, they are better placed to ask the questions that will explain them.

The above may be a route to the age-old question of how many angels can dance on the head of a pin but there are pragmatic and easily understood examples of this process in action. Faced with the difficulty of writing a travelogue confined to those strips of British land that qualify as neither rural or urban and exist beyond the boundaries of commercial use Michael Symmons Roberts and Paul Farley titled their book Edgelands. The term pithily engaging with the mystery of what exactly these places are if they're not recognised as built or rural environments. Like many works that use creativity to explore an issue, Edgelands is essentially a meditation on places widely misunderstood and little regarded. Its beauty as a book revolves around the way it weaves a combination of fact and imagination to explore a new reality. It's both a creative exercise and an academic enquiry (certainly in the sense in which works of art might qualify as academic enquiries). It also highlights the way mystery can become a very practical element of our expanding knowledge because it provides a snapshot of some of the edgelands, but in doing so invites us to think about spaces we seldom consider. It highlights strange collisions of activity and insights into a community to be found in such places – notably in one scene where amateur astronomers are seizing the opportunity to stargaze at the end of an unlit deserted road on an industrial estate whilst nearby sex workers are waiting for cars.

Creative works exploring nebulous ideas show us that questioning as we learn is often most effective when it tests the limits of our understanding. When we dissolve any idea of the limits of our own capabilities, we create a minor mystery concerning what comes next. We might have clear ideas of what might occur, but we don't know. In the case of a book like Edgelands, the act of adopting a little used word and employing it to define a terrain previously described by other terms is also a small venture into mystery. The precise use of term edgelands is credited to writer and environmental campaigner Marion Shoard and dated to 2002. Critics and academics often talk in terms of re-imagining or needing a new language. In a very practical sense, the invention of a new word and the use of it to begin such an exploration is an act of self-belief and an acceptance of mystery. The first thing a new word invites is meditative thought about what makes the edgelands unique and how our understanding of
13

them can be developed. Thinking and exploring without a clear goal other than greater understanding is one of the ways we all invite mystery into our lives every day. We often explain it in different terms of wanting to find out or being curious. But our experiences in testing new ideas – whether academically or simply because we feel a need to try something are our entry in mystery, even if they are sometimes on a mundane level. Without mystery, all life runs the risk of being mundane all the time.

All mystery, whether created for us to enjoy, presented as proof of something beyond our understanding or simply experienced in a surprising life event can be fascinating. We frequently express this fascination in conversations and contact with others. So, mystery matters to almost all of us for almost all of the time. We share our experience of mystery and investigate those mysteries we think may have most importance to our lives. We do not take time very often to consider mystery in isolation. Mystery as a thing itself.

This book is here to argue that valuing mystery for its own sake is vitally important, possibly more so than it has been in living memory. Specifically, mystery matters for three highly important reasons:

1 – Embracing the biggest mysteries is key to us understanding who we are and what purposes we can find in life.

2 – Mystery is key to us developing significant new knowledge for use in our lives and key to those experiences that shape us and give a sense of direction to our day-to-day lives.

3 – Mystery, in the way we have learned to value it to promote a deeper understanding of ourselves is now massively under threat. Certainly, in the western world. The way the internet and in particular social media understand and interact with us means we are frequently fed information presenting itself as certainty, or facts presenting themselves as the end of an argument. Mystery itself is too nebulous for many of those managing our online interactions.

This short book sets out to address the three points above and leave enough in the way of information and ideas to allow you to manage your own journey from there. I hope our journey together will be informative, and that it will bring some emotional impact and occasional humour. Mystery matters most when we feel it. To reduce it to words and examples is dishonest and only a partial exploration of why mystery matters. So, this book is a start, nothing more.

# CHAPTER TWO

# THE BIGGEST MYSTERIES

"Maybe the point of life is to give up certainty and to embrace life's beautiful uncertainty." Matt Haig: Notes on a Nervous Plane

A well-known though not always well understood joke is central to the first of the books in the Hitchhiker's Guide to the Galaxy series. In answer to the big question of what "life, the Universe and everything" actually means a supercomputer designed solely for the purposes of solving this conundrum deliberates to the point of leaving those waiting for the reply in a state of profound agitation before delivering the answer; "42." The number, at once mundane and enigmatic is the only response offered. In the writing of this scene author Douglas

Adams considered other numbers — including reversing the digits to read 24 — before deciding 42 simply felt right in terms of providing the right comedy value. Quoting the number has been an in-joke for aficionados of the book series, radio series and movie franchise since the late seventies when the work first appeared. Casual fans and those who have heard the story at second hand frequently miss the whole context. In the original story the computer charged with providing the answer is called Deep Thought, those programming it are identified as "hyperintelligent, pan-dimensional beings," and the riddle of what "life the universe and everything" might mean is described as the "Ultimate Question." All of which provides good comedy when the computer answers accurately and those seeking the answer haven't a clue what the thing they most wanted actually means. Theories of comedy suggest we laugh most readily when the joke confronting us presents something incongruous, allows us to feel some sense of superiority or surprises us. The "42" joke bundles up all three of those comedy qualities. It's an incongruous answer because to our minds it doesn't even address the question, the superiority element is a comedy basic and resembles many jokes in which we see someone prepare meticulously before failing spectacularly, and with the timing on the page and in the radio and filmed adaptions the surprise element is delivered effectively.

In the Hitchhiker's Guide story, the moment is also pivotal because Deep Thought goes on to offer some solace to the hyperintelligent, pan-dimensional beings by tactfully pointing out that they didn't know how to ask that Ultimate Question. They required more information and specifically a computer that could help them devise that question sufficiently well to provide the answer they wanted. Deep Thought offers to help in the design of the computer and the Hitchhiker's Guide soon reveals that the computer devised for just this purpose is Planet Earth. However, by the time we reach this point in the Hitchhiker's Guide story we are already aware that the Earth has been destroyed because the opening scenes of the story involve our unlikely and understated hero, Arthur Dent, being rescued by his friend Ford Prefect just before an alien race called the Vogons demolish the entire planet to make way for a hyperspace bypass. Crudely, the best computer ever designed and all the secrets it contains are obliterated for little more than improving the local traffic system.

The massive joke under-pinning the action in the Hitchhiker's Guide series is funny because it goes to the heart of the way many of us experience the search for the deepest truths in our life. Simply knowing how to construct the question is a major problem. The mystery of who we are, whether there is any purpose to our existence, and whether any of it matters gnaws away at us – sometimes to the point of distracting us from everything else we might want to do. Many of us also fear the answers we might get, were we ever able to ask the big questions. The experience of mystery as something ever present is part of the human condition. It can inject a regular restlessness into life. Mystery is endemic to us, knowing how to use and channel our experience of mystery is less common.

The experience of the mysterious and frequently the kind of personal experience we describe as mystic has been central to the religious experiences and teaching that have guided our race to the present day. Considered from a purely secular point of view the development of our religions often demonstrates that mystery plays a central part in their teachings and their ability to reach out and gain a following. From one perspective it could be argued that little has changed fundamentally from the start of recorded time to now because all that mankind has succeeded in doing is observing, experiencing mysteries as we do. In that scenario we have understood some of the

20

mysteries through investigation but realized in doing so that they lead us on to greater mysteries. That pattern is central to works like Reza Aslan's God: A Human History of Religion (2017) which suggests our spiritual beliefs may be an "accidental byproduct" of the need to unite and achieve common goals. In this version of events the important work of religion lies in giving us common purposes and bringing us together to achieve goals that help a society, or societies. Reza Aslan sums up the work of some of the anthropologists and evolutionary scientists who have examined the growth of religion from mystic rituals linked to the needs of mankind to its present-day state with the observation; "Religion, they say, is not an evolutionary adaptation; religion is an accidental byproduct of some other *preexisting* evolutionary adaptation." [Aslan's italics]. [1]

Stephen Hawking was an atheist who saw no evidence of the universe being created to serve any specific purpose. His narration in the opening episode of the Discovery Channel's series, Curiosity included the observation; "We are each free to believe what we want and it is my view that the simplest explanation is there is no God. No one created the universe and no one directs our fate. This leads me to a profound realisation. There is probably

21

no heaven, and no afterlife either. We have this one life to appreciate the grand design of the universe, and for that, I am extremely grateful."

Leonard Mlodinow co-authored The Grand Design (2010) with Hawking, a work which expanded on Hawking's theories about the origins of the universe. Writing in a memoir of his friendship with Hawking in 2020 Mlodinow expanded on Hawking's claims in The Grand Design, noting that he and Hawking had disagreed about a headline claim in the work. Hawking was insistent on stating "philosophy is dead," Mlodinow suggested a more tactful phrase that took current human behaviour into account; "as a way of understanding the physical world, philosophy is dead." Hawking wouldn't budge, mindful, perhaps of the marketing possibilities of his curt expression but also certain in his own view that theoretical physics had surpassed philosophy as the means by which mankind confronted and investigated the most fundamental mysteries concerning, well; life, the universe and everything.

Other significant thinkers on the same subject have developed different beliefs in the face of studying quantum theory. A leading advocate of deterministic ideas suggesting there may be purpose and design in the universe is Gerard t'Hooft, winner of the Nobel

Prize in Physics in 1999. T'Hooft wryly noted that his 2016 work "The Cellular Automaton Interpretation of Quantum Mechanics" arguing the possibilities of a purposeful universe received mixed reactions. "Purposeful" in the sense that some quantum theorists recognize it is a fluid concept with one extreme seeing just a universe that operates like a machine, programmed to self-regulate and another area of thought wondering if the mysteries we constantly encounter come our way because some supreme intelligence guides us but remains out of sight. A succinct consideration of this conundrum appears in Robert Macfarlane's award-winning Underland; a travelogue largely devoted to journeys under the ground. Macfarlane visits Boulby in Yorkshire, a very deep mine which also provides the perfect conditions for physicists to investigate dark matter because only a very few particles can penetrate to a depth of half a mile under the surface of the Earth. Macfarlane quotes Rebecca Elson, a dark matter physicist and poet who likens the task of detecting particles and using the discoveries to guide our understanding of the universe to discovering fireflies and using that discovery to "infer the meadow."

Macfarlane also meets Christopher who sees his task of searching for dark matter in a deep mine as worthwhile partly because it can "give life meaning. If we're not exploring, we're not doing anything. We're just waiting." Christopher's Christian upbringing taught him a lot about faith, but he lost his faith having discovered physics only to re-discover faith "in a much-changed form." As he explains the situation "No divinity in which I would wish to believe would declare itself by means of what we would recognize as evidence…If there is a god, we should not be able to find it. If I detected proof of a deity, I would distrust that deity on the grounds that a god should be smarter than that."

Christopher is arguing the value of mystery and its ability to give meaning to his life. Ultimately, it is a statement of faith. Coming from a physicist engaged in a cutting-edge project to understand the make-up of the cosmos it has a gravity we should take seriously. But, in other aspects this faith resembles a record of celebrating mystery and mysticism that is as old as archaeology can prove any human activity to be, possibly older. If, as some claim, there is religious or mystical significance in a small stone discovered in Israel in 1981 and known as the Berekhat Ram then our celebration of the mystic goes back to before humans in their current incarnation as a species existed. The Berekhat Ram remains controversial. Claims that a few significant marks have modified an existing stone to represent a female figure are disputed by many. There is less dispute about the fact that ritual burial sites of Homo Sapiens date back at least 100,000 years. Some see this as a conservative estimate and the mere presence of multiple remains in older sites, like the Zhoukoudian cave system near Beijing (which includes the site of discovery of Peking Man) suggest that our ancestors grouped bodies together for some ritual purpose a few hundreds of thousands of years ago. Prehistoric cave paintings have proven to have impact indentations, suggesting that our very distant ancestors depicted animals with some ritual or mystic intent – possibly stabbing the representations with spears in some ceremonial enactment of a hunt.

The archaeological record is fragmentary and some experts, notably Alaistair Pike, Professor of Archaeological Sciences at the University of Southampton, have expressed the opinion that many artistic expressions placed in the landscape have probably been lost to time and the elements; suggesting that the cave art we have is a fragment of what once existed. However, it is notable that such art exists on every continent apart from Antarctica and its most significant expressions – such as the works in the Lascaux caves in France – are on a truly epic scale. The French caves include very particular depictions of animals including a wounded Bison and a bird on a stick. Most cave works were created in conditions that demanded the best artificial lighting available, which would have involved burning substances like animal fat with a rudimentary wick.

*The Berekhat Ram*

The effort to create such works far from daylight and other people, and then bring others to experience them would have been considerable; suggesting the works would only have been created because they served a significant purpose. Researchers including Chantal Conneller – an expert on the Mesolithic period – have noted that art produced by humans develops an iconic quality from around 20,000 years ago.

Understanding the purposes of the fragmentary finds we have from humanity's distant past will always be limited by the lack of a written record and the randomness of the evidence now discoverable. What we can safely say is that there is no epoch of the known history of our species that appears to be free of some ritual enactments inspired by mankind's wish to understand and control the mysterious. These enactments and the depictions left to us also show a progress, certainly where our investigation of mystery is concerned. The art we have moves from figurative to iconic with abstract shapes and partial depictions serving a purpose. Along the way the focus of our attention may have changed according to our needs. Reza Aslan noted; "Hunting may have made us human, but farming forever altered what being human meant. If hunting gave us mastery over space, farming forced us to master time, to synchronize the movements of the stars and the Sun with the agricultural cycle." [2] The archaeological record offers evidence of ritual sites linked to hunting and agriculture with different cultures in their own ways offering up sacrifices, erecting places of worship and attempting to create a space fit to share with their gods. The trading of effort and attention on the part of humans for benevolence and good fortune provided by gods spans cultures. The varied sites and temples constructed have often become a strong focus of the lives lived in a particular area. The manpower required to build a monument on the scale of Stonehenge still amazes us; with a consistently popular but unevidenced claim being that such an achievement was only possible with the help of aliens from space. The archaeological record suggests otherwise, with evidence of continued activity in that area of Salisbury Plain over a prolonged period and chemical analysis now helping us locate the original source of the stones.

Historically, many of the most effective lines of worship across cultures combine the qualities of being human with extraordinary abilities demonstrated in front of worshippers but offering some mysterious element by way of the powers demonstrated. Shamanic powers allowed individuals to commune with gods. Gods themselves were presented as humanoid but possessed of greater abilities. Rituals frequently employed behaviour designed to cause sensory disturbance in those attending. One clear example of this occurred during the final struggles between native American Indians and white settlers for control of The United States. The religious leader Wovoka (known to white Americans as Jack Wilson) was already established as a spiritual authority with extraordinary powers which were reputed to include control of the weather. He had reportedly brought about the miraculous materialisation of ice falling from a warm summer sky. During a solar eclipse on New Year's Day 1889 Wovoka fell into a coma. The cause of the coma would later be claimed by some to be scarlet fever, but Wovoka experienced a vision which united and inspired the beaten and bedraggled remains of the native tribes. Wovoka's vision involved the resurrection of the dead of his own Paiute people. The tribe had once seen much of America's great basin area as their own lands; roaming across California, Nevada, and Oregon. By 1889 the lands were much prized as the white population spread west and settled where they could farm, hunt and prospect. Wovoka's vision suggested the resurrected Paiute dead would help the living rid their lands of the new settlers and restore the order the tribe had previously enjoyed. Wovoka informed his people these events would come to pass once they had learned a new dance.

*Wovoka*

Whilst similar to some traditional dances the new Ghost Dance was innovative in its scale – particularly the length of time spent dancing - and the claims made for its ability to turn the tide in a war. Its power was infectious among the tribes to the point Dee Brown's classic Bury my Heart at Wounded Knee later noted "Ghost Dancing was so prevalent on the Sioux reservations that almost all other activities came to a halt." The name "Ghost Dance" came from white settlers who found the spectacle frightening. The numbers involved and the widespread knowledge that minor variations of the dance were spreading throughout the land also scared the settlers. A central claim of Wovoka's prophecy was that the dance, the involvement of dead ancestors and the wearing of special shirts would protect the native Americans from bullets and ensure victory in a dispute they were clearly losing by 1889.

The involvement of massive numbers in the dance and the sense of living a prophecy did bring resolve and power back to the native Americans. The fight ended tragically for them with the massacre at Wounded Knee on 29 December 1890. Somewhere between 250 and 300 Lakota, many of them women and children and many of the men already having surrendered their weapons, were killed by gun and cannon fire from the American cavalry. [3] The growth of the Ghost Dance demonstrates the way mystery and other major elements of religious experience can appear from within a community. It is a phenomenon known and understood by theologists, those who study religion. A key element within this being the way an element of mystery – in this case Wovoka's prophecy - can be shared and enacted in a manner that allows others within a group to feel their own personal involvement. The same behaviour is seen in churches when people testify about the power of God in their lives, but also in groups united around paranormal phenomena. This channelling of mystery (by way of a spiritual force that appears to exist beyond the normal laws of physics) allows a group to transcend their reality, feel close to a greater power and at the same time develop a view of the world that belittles the problems they face and present themselves with some model of perfection, salvation, and the sense of a spiritual existence beyond the present.

Anthropologists have written detailed accounts of this from many perspectives, identifying the key role of the experience of mystery as a focal point for the experiences of the groups they observe. Tragic endings, like those at Wounded Knee or the mass suicide of 39 members of the Heaven's Gate group members in 1997 who died – apparently – sure of their own resurrection aboard a UFO trailing the Hale Bopp comet as it passed the Earth, are relatively rare. In many cases the common element of mystery, exemplified by the presence of people sharing mysterious experience, and involving others in some element of this, is enough to sustain a group over a long period. I can share a personal experience of this having once taken part in a mass session to generate prayer energy. The group responsible were the Aetherius Society. Their belief system suggests the major religious teachers in our history including Jesus and Buddha were really beings from other planets, here to provide guidance. The group see their founder – George King – as another master in the tradition of the major figures who founded the world's most enduring religions. Aetherians sometimes meet on mountains and chant mantras, including those familiar to Buddhists. One notable operation in their history – Operation Prayer Power – used prayer energy to charge batteries and sought to release the energy to help our own planet in times of trouble. I don't share Aetherian beliefs but I was writing something about them earlier this century and their invitation for me to join a prayer session on Holdstone Down in Devon, a sacred site to them, was warm and sincere. The lengthy chanting session was bound to be uplifting given the scenery and the breathing required to maintain an extended chant for much of an afternoon. Nothing motivated me to join the Aetherians but I spoke to professional people and members who clearly led focussed and happy lives. Any disagreement I might have with their belief system was offset by the fact the lives of the people I met that afternoon had a level of spiritual certainty lacking in my own life. Once again, it's a matter of faith and in the case of the Aetherians a major element in sustaining that faith is the history of the group receiving direct messages from space beings and the faith held by members that a new Master will come to Earth once the planet has moved itself to a spiritual position worthy of receiving that visit. In receiving these teachings and sharing the experience of preparing the way for the new Master all Aetherians can feel close enough to mystery to be able to experience it in their own lives. This pattern is much more typical of small religious groups around the world than are the more spectacular but newsworthy events, like Heaven's Gate suicides.

Often, it's the sense of mystery that matters to hold groups together and provide a purpose. The physicist – Christopher – encountered by Robert Macfarlane half a mile under the ground in north Yorkshire finished his discussion with the author with a down to earth statement about mystery. Employed to search out evidence for dark matter and thoughtful about religion to the point he wouldn't trust any god that chose to reveal itself he still counted these elements of his life as less impactful than an everyday mystery most of us encounter. "Mostly, and in several ways, I'm amazed I'm able to hold the hand of the person I love." [4] In that statement it is obvious that humanity may have moved significantly in its ability to ask questions and investigate mystery, but some mysterious experiences remain timeless and central to our experience of being human. Romantic love is mysterious, but it's also a force and set of beliefs central to the operation of many societies. Every time people testify and share to this experience – for example by inviting others to their wedding – they may be aiming to bring those people close to the experience of that mystery.

In recent years our abilities to locate and map the neural pathways of the brain have given us an insight into how we experience mystery. Some investigations have focussed specifically on how we experience religion. One investigation at UCLA in 2007 set out to "differentiate belief, disbelief, and uncertainty at the level of the brain." Crudely, to identify the differences in our processing of things believed and things disbelieved. A summary of the findings on the website of one of the researchers – Sam Harris – notes; "While many areas of higher cognition are likely involved in assessing the truth-value of linguistic propositions, the final acceptance of a statement as 'true,' or its rejection as 'false,' seems to rely on more primitive, hedonic processing in the medial prefrontal cortex and the anterior insula. Truth may be beauty, and beauty truth, in more than a metaphorical sense, and false propositions might actually disgust us." The findings of the study included evidence that the mental effort involved in disbelief is significantly greater than believing something. The study discovered – amongst other things – that Christians displayed a stronger signal in their prefrontal brain region than non-believers when faced with questions about God and the Virgin Birth. In plain English, studies like that at UCLA help us to understand that belief in something may be a natural state for humans and that gathering and processing information into a pattern that makes sense is often a process of lining up a logical argument in our brain and experiencing a sense of that pattern simply feeling right. Sam Harris' observation – "Truth may be beauty, and beauty truth, in more than a metaphorical sense" – is an elegant expression of something central to the human condition.

Considered in this context our brains are adapted to help us make sense of the world, and the greatest sense comes when the subjective and objective both seem to exist peacefully in the same place. We are adapted to build and hold beliefs. Some studies have focussed specifically on the notion of a "God slot" in the human brain, predisposing us to belief. Understanding our experience of religion remains an active and contentious area of research. At one extreme, there is a clear argument that the "accidental byproduct" model of religion simply fits with the way we have evolved to reason and believe. By contrast anyone seeing our propensity to believe as proof of intervention by a higher intelligence can find their faith strengthened by every mystic experience, because they see the brain's ability to process our faith as a gift from God. In 1902 William James' epic investigation of The Varieties of Religious Experience set a benchmark for studies that continues to be influential. James opened his account with a chapter on Religion and Neurology, a gesture that set him apart from most of the leading scientific and theological thinkers of his day. He was motivated partly by a desire to distance himself from some popular and lucrative practices of the time; notably the fashion for seances offered by the highly successful "Spiritualist" movement. But his

37

willingness to explore consciousness and the nature of mystic experience brought him into areas which remain central to our understanding of mystery. Divided into lectures James' work dives deeply into each nuance of its subject and is notable for the enthusiasm with which he interrogates topics like the experience of religious conversion. James helped establish much of the language and many of the central ideas we still use to understand the religious experience, and mystery. He is credited with helping to define concepts like stream of consciousness which became hugely influential on the cultural movements of the early twentieth century. In devoting two lectures to mysticism James set out a template that has informed a range of research in areas as diverse as psychology and understanding the meaning of the new age movements.

In a section dealing with "four marks of mystic states" James defines the mystic experience. The first marker of such a state being it presenting something ineffable; "more like states of feeling than states of intellect." Put simply, something experienced in a way that is hard to express. James uses the experience of listening to a symphony or falling in love as analogies. The second mark of a mystic state is a "noetic quality" or "states of knowledge." Apparently at odds with the ineffability James is precise enough to explore this quality and make clear he is talking about "illuminations, revelations, full of significance and importance." The revelations reported at Fatima, fifteen years after James' book was published might count as examples in this case. The third mark of a mystic state is its transiency. Such states can't be sustained for long and "Often, when faded, their quality can but imperfectly be reproduced in memory." The final marker is passivity where "the mystic feels as if his own will were in abeyance." This is true regardless of whether a significant preparation has been undertaken, as a shaman might attempt before entering a mystical state, or whether someone has unwittingly and immediately entered a mystic state. In conclusion James notes "The simplest rudiment of a mystical experience would seem to be that deepened sense of significance of a maxim or formula which occasionally sweeps over one." [5] Quite simply, James acknowledges that mystic states can find us even if we aren't necessarily looking for them and the impact is significant but also largely beyond our ability to control. The end result is that we may feel changed and may well feel as if some element of knowledge or greater awareness has been given to us.

A recent overview of research into our religious and mystical experiences points out that "no one after

[William] James has followed through on his idea that spiritual experience, particularly mystical experience, could be a conscious state in its own right." The reason for this being "when we have considered spiritual experience it has been viewed as the stuff of waking consciousness, the product of thalmus and cortex." [6]

A summary of the observations above and much of the neuroscience that has been done on the subject makes clear that we often examine mystic states – which are for many people the most intense experiences of mystery they will ever know – as a gateway experience. Much of what is written and discussed about them highlights either the changes resulting from our experiences or the possible purpose of the experience. For example, considering whether a deity or higher intelligence was behind the experience. In many cases the people experiencing such states understand them in this manner. The popularisation of psychedelic exploration by way of taking drugs like LSD in the 1960's relied to some extent on those experienced in taking trips acting as evangelists, as in the case of leaders of the movement like Timothy Leary or initiates as in the case of many others. Their experiences of raised consciousness and sudden moments of awareness of the connectedness of all things suggested there was an easily and accessible route anyone could take to reach revelations. Crudely, that there was a short cut to the experiences typically imparted by religious figures like The Buddha. The same movement led to an increase in research into the neurological nature of a mystic state. The uses, and abuses of such states became the subject of a massive literature. The nightmare stories included the massive use of psychedelic drugs in the Manson Family (the group of a few dozen young people surrounding ex-convict Charles Manson who went on to carry out a notorious series of murders in California). The more numerous positive stories recounted during the period suggested psychedelic drugs greatly enhanced creativity and deepened a range of sensory experiences.

Mystery mattered in such cases largely because it appeared to last long enough to be explored and experienced in some depth. The popular psychedelic movement never died out and went on to morph into a range of disparate beliefs which were often crudely lumped together under banners like "New Age." Along with the ongoing testifying of those in a range of religious communities, the literature of the New Age provides much evidence that the experience of mystery, and the mystic is a gateway for many to a sense of understanding our place regarding the Ultimate Question.

The left hemisphere of the primate brain controls language and reasoning and is notably more developed in human beings than other species of primate. More than any other species humans can discuss and record our mysterious experiences gradually distilling them into narratives that contain meaning. Processing this information into memories occurs when the large array of neural links becomes involved. Long-term memories have a physical presence in the brain because they are formed when neurons make connections. Such memories exist whether they are regularly used, or not. We can recall, reflect, and build a bank of memories over a lifetime. The events that test us in life, including massive challenges like threats to our life produce a surge of information from the brain stem. This travels to the amygdala and onwards to a range of destinations, notably those within our limbic system that impact on our emotional responses and memories, meaning some memories are charged with emotion.

At the other end of our experience are those instances of brief emotional response and mild sense of mystery; for example, noticing a shaft of sunlight as it brings about a minor change of mood. Between these extremes of pleasant moments and those sudden events that induce a sense of our lives being vulnerable we generate much of the mental material that maps our personal view of the answer to the Ultimate Question.

As we have seen, the mental effort involved in generating disbelief is greater than that involved in believing something. Those moments of mystery when our perceptions are challenged or ambushed are vital to the build-up of our view of the cosmos. We can choose how often and how aggressively we seek out mystery. But even those most prone to avoiding the mysterious are likely to be regularly faced with it. The challenge of distilling our deepest beliefs often faces us when our emotional or physical well-being is threatened. We are likely to face this challenge whatever our religious beliefs might be. For example, we may well appreciate some organised ceremony as we experience a bereavement. Whether such a ceremony is devoutly religious or completely secular it still tends to be based around statements that make meaning about the life of the deceased and its importance to the living who mourn that person. Frequently the preparations for a funeral involve refining some sense of certainty from the mix of emotions and memories we have about a particular person. Much of the same mental machinery used to engage in making sense of the life of a person we have lost is the same machinery we use when mystery ambushes us.

Mystery matters in these moments because the alternative to engaging with uncertainty is an emotional shutdown that does few favours to anyone. Shutting down and caving under an emotional load engages fewer neural pathways than being more open. It's also a short route to generating the "stress hormone" cortisol.

We have no definitive proof of whether evolution, intelligent design, or a combination of both brought about our talents for experiencing mystery. We have choices about how we interpret our experiences. Recently, we have developed a body of research that gives us all some insights into experiences of the mysterious and how they might teach us all something about our lives and our experiences of anything that may exist beyond our lives. Firstly, we should note that the role of our brain in interpreting some of the most mundane information can create the most extreme mental states. Whilst these don't strictly involve the experience of mystery, they do provide examples of the role of the brain in making sense of our surroundings. An exceptionally strange condition – Cotard's Syndrome – remains listed in the standard diagnostic manual for mental health, the DSM. First comprehensively described by the neurologist Jules Cotard in 1880 and expressed as "The Delirium of Negation" the condition involves individuals who claim not to exist. Sufferers exist in a truly paradoxical state in which they experience themselves as dead or in some state of non-existence. Their living senses have been known to feed messages to their brain confirming their death. A patient known to Cotard believed her combined state of life and death was the result of her having died and being doomed to eternal damnation; thereby being entombed in the body she had known in life. Identified in the clinical literature as Mademoiselle X, she resisted treatment to the point of succeeding in starving herself to death. Other Cotard's sufferers have been known experience the smell of their own putrefying flesh.

Thankfully most of us will never experience such capabilities of processing information and interpreting it in ways at odds with the realities shared by most other humans. But conditions like Cotard's prove that the brain's role is central to shaping our experience of the mysterious. Cultural values and other variables clearly play a part. One area of ongoing mystery and debate concerns near death experiences (NDEs). Many people who have experienced the state known as clinical death describe a range of similar experiences. These frequently involve feelings of peace and some encounter with a bright light, and people already known to have died.. One of the most prolific researchers and writers on the subject – Raymond Moody – runs the lifeafterlife website and has published a series of books. Many researchers dispute the reliability of his findings and take issue with a methodology that relies greatly on interviews and collecting stories, but the sincerity of many of the accounts is another matter. People encounter the mysterious in near-death states and others witnessing those on the brink of death also see and hear enough to verify some of the things reported. Some of the cases do appear to be informed by the cultural experiences of people in life. One case reported by Moody concerns a girl with Downs Syndrome called Jennifer who died with her parents at her bedside. Raised by Elvis fans and familiar with the star and his music to the extent she attended one Elvis show as a very young girl, Jennifer died in 1980. Quoting Jennifer's mother Moody reports; "She said 'Love you Mummy and Dimmy.' Then she said, 'Here comes Elvis.' She was holding her arms out like she was trying to reach toward someone and hug them. She said it twice. 'Here comes Elvis.' Then she collapsed and died. She had the most beautiful smile on her face as she died." [7]

21st century investigations into near death experience suggest common aspects and sensations, including seeing a brilliant white light and a sense of peace and unity with things. Intriguingly researchers like Kevin Nelson at the University of Kentucky have discovered those reporting a near death experience often exhibit quite low instances of reports of the paranormal, such as being able to perceive the future. Nelson concludes; "As we collected accounts…it was clear that each one was shaped by life experience, cultural background and individual and shared biology." [8]

Paranormal encounters with figures like Elvis have been widely reported and fall into a lengthy history of mystic experiences. This history presents beings who were human to the extent of being able to communicate with us but also paranormal in their ability to reach us from outside the physical realm. Clearly, many others would dispute whether Elvis was anything more than human, but those reporting mystic experiences linked to figures like Elvis generally do so in all sincerity. Many psychics report using a spirit guide and those associated with mysticism – especially religious mystics – encounter divine figures. Margery Kempe (c. 1373 – c. 1438) was celebrated as a religious mystic but also frequently suspected of heresy. Her encounters with Jesus Christ are recorded in The Book of Margery Kempe. Some assessments of Kempe's mysticism suggest a severe episode of post-partum psychosis might explain the visions that came to define her life. Initially overwhelmed with demons and devils, Kempe carried out acts of self-harm and was probably suicidal before Christ himself appeared; prompting a series of encounters that brought Kempe to the devout mysticism that made her a celebrity. Kempe is known to have had 14 children and may have had more given the prevalence of still-births at the time. Her vivid accounts of the mystic experiences that continued throughout her life frequently cite sensory experiences including smelling and hearing things. She was venerated in her own lifetime and influential, particularly as an advocate for the rights of women. Kempe encouraged some women towards celibacy and living independently. Contemporary reports cast her as a woman at odds with much of the normal behaviour of the time. Despite her many children she dressed in virginal white when she went on pilgrimages. Her fellow pilgrims were motivated to force her out. She often ate on the margins of the group and was generally shunned. Significant religious figures of the time – however – entertained her, and she overcame the heresy allegations by convincing some senior Catholics of her sincerity and authenticity.

Margery Kempe's life story was known to have been compiled into a book from which quotes had been taken for other works. The unexpected find of a complete manuscript in 1934 allowed the full account to re-emerge. From our current perspective, focussing on the experience of mystery the combination of sincerity and the uncanny experiences described puts Kempe's tale firmly into the model presented by William James. Kempe is unusual only in that her spiritual encounters with Jesus, and others (God himself at times), occurred over a long period.

I have met many highly sincere people who reported mysteries. After a lifetime of paranormal interest, writing and live speaking I've come to value the truly bizarre cases which are often overlooked by the best-selling literature and best performing documentaries on the subject. In terms of provable sincerity, it would be hard to beat one man I met briefly who had a strange event to report. The details of his story bore some resemblance to a famous case from the UK in 1978 in which Ken Edwards, a 39-year-old service engineer returning from a union meeting, had an encounter with a mysterious being near an atomic facility in Risley, Cheshire and appeared to lose the best part of an hour from his life. The man I met had clearly been shaken by his own experience and wasn't remotely interested in selling his story because his first request was that anyone investigating his case didn't tell his wife (not that there was anything to hide beyond his own worries about how much the experience had under-mined his sense of himself as a strong person). The study of UFOs, sometimes called ufology, has a steady stream of truly mysterious tales which appear to exist in cul-de-sacs of the surreal. Such stories seldom match each other. In 1983 retired soldier Alfred Burtoo was fishing next to the Basingstoke canal in the early hours when he saw a UFO land and soon met two beings from the craft who shepherded him aboard. At this point a voice from a creature he didn't see enquired about his age. Burtoo announced he would be 78 on his next birthday and was promptly told; "You are too old and infirm for our purpose." He returned to fishing and watched the UFO take off shortly afterwards. Burtoo did go public, but only to his local paper and mainly to seek any other witnesses to the strange event. Nobody came forward to corroborate his story, but he remained adamant it had happened.

After his death his widow continued to state his account was sincere. Some years later his story was compiled as part of a massive-selling book. By then, Burtoo was dead.

Taken literally Alfred Burtoo's story suggests an alien spacecraft came all the way to Hampshire. We might usefully surmise the technological ability to get there meant any creatures on board would be scientifically advanced in comparison to humans. However, they were seemingly unable to tell whether a 77-year-old man was a suitable specimen for whatever they had in mind until they brought him on board and asked him his age. Other surreal accounts I have come to value include a case from Rowley Regis in the west midlands in which entities floated into and around a house during the Christmas holidays and the only occupant of the house at the time offered them mince pies. Another intriguing case from Australia involves a woman who had a history of mysterious encounters agreeing to meet UFO researchers and encountering an alien at the same time as the meeting took place. A significant twist in this case being that the witness – Maureen Puddy – saw an alien walk around a car but the same alien remained invisible to both UFO researchers in attendance.

Such stories resemble the centuries of fairy-lore known and shared in many western countries. I noted in another of my books; "Many themes which would subsequently become staples of UFO cases consistently appear in tales of the fairy kingdom…many attempts to remove items from the fairy kingdom as proof of a visit appear to come to grief. The beings from the kingdom seem able to shape-shift and often appear in unfamiliar and confusing disguises. Time spent in the realm of these elemental beings may pass at a different rate to time for those left behind. In one case from Wales a man missing for three weeks believed he had only been gone for three hours. Messages gathered from the fairy kingdom may be contradictory and predictions have a tendency to amount to nothing. However, despite these problems, there is a peculiar consistency. The people contacted are often left clinging to stories which do them no favours in terms of their credibility." [9]

One mystery that exists firmly on the fringes of fairy lore and ufology is the case of Joe Simonton. The chicken farmer from Eagle River, Wisconsin, spent some strange minutes on 18 April 1961 doing the bidding of a trio of small men inside a shiny craft. He gave them water and they gifted him a few rough and tasteless pancakes. Subsequent analysis of one

52

pancake by the Food and Drug Laboratory of the US Department of Health, Education and Welfare declared the pancake "of terrestrial origin." Simonton had support from physicist J Allen Hynek – believed by many to be the greatest ever ufologist - who concluded; "There is no question that Mr Simonton felt that his contact had been a real experience." Hynek believed a waking dream state to be the likely explanation of the case. We all experience waking dream states. Hypnagogia, is the technical term for such a state as we sink into sleep. It's partner – hypnopompic – state occurs as we wake. In these moments of being half awake and half asleep a range of phenomena can occur including lucid dreams combining some things in our surroundings and thoughts from within our brains and states of conscious paralysis. At these times we can experience weird events we may subsequently remember as if they really occurred. In one sense they do because such events are grounded in the realities of when and where they occur, places like Joe Simonton's farm, for instance.

To some of the more sceptically minded investigators of a range of paranormal claims the lucid dream states are an obvious explanation for encounters with ghosts, aliens, fairies, and a range of other uncanny and incredible claims reported by

53

sincere people. In the context of a consideration of mystery, they at least demonstrate a link between the deepest recesses of human consciousness and events we can experience as lucid reality.

Joe Simonton didn't ask for his strange encounter, but humanity's history of mystery includes instances of many who made questing into the mysterious both a fashion and a tradition. Notable creative artists in all disciplines have explored the dream states in search of enlightenment and meaning. With each succeeding generation inspired by the works that have gone before in areas like painting, music and writing we have bodies of work rich in representations of mystery. Margery Kempe was one of a group of writers eventually categorized as the "medieval mystics." Their work offering religious interpretations of encounters with nature and visitations of supernatural forces. John Donne combined preaching and poetry. He had a paranormal experience whilst on a diplomatic visit to Paris. Having left his wife heavily pregnant and reluctant to part from him, Donne saw her in Paris pass by him twice "with her hair hanging about her shoulders and a dead child in her arms." Donne persuaded his patron, Sir Robert Dudley, to despatch a servant back to London and it was confirmed Anne Donne had indeed suffered a miscarriage.

Anne Donne survived but died following another stillbirth in 1619. Five years later, ill to the point he was convinced his own death was close Donne threw himself into the frenzied writing of Devotions Upon Emergent Occasions (1624). His work is a stark exploration of his illness and the attempts by physicians to cure him with the best options at hand – including applying pigeons "to draw vapours from the head." Observing the failure of his senses, he considers human frailty: "Man, who is the noblest part of the earth, melts so away, as if he were a statue, not of earth, but of snow. We see his own envy melts him, he grows lean with that; he will say, another's beauty melts him; but he feels that a fever doth not melt him like snow, but pour him out like lead, like iron, like brass melted in a furnace; it doth not only melt him, but calcine him, reduce him to atoms, and to ashes; not to water, but to lime. And how quickly?" [12] He recovered, eventually dying in 1631 though his thoughts on mortality remained a major part of his writing. "Death, it would seem, was seldom far from his imagination." [13] Donne found a mystical rapture in his regular meditations on human weakness next to divine strength.

Mystery and mysticism in creative art often finds those occasions when the senses are overwhelmed. Other mystical writers have become lost in the moment – a classic rapture appears in Roger Ascham's Toxophilus (1545); "the winde was whistelinge a lofte, and sharp accordynge to the tyme of the yeare. The snowe in the hye waye lay lowse and troden with horse feete: so as the wynde blewe, it toke the lowse fnow with it, and made it so slide upon the snowe in the felde whyche was harde and crufted by reason of the frost ouer nyght, that thereby I myght fe verye wel, the hole nature of the wynde as it blew yat daye." Surrendering to the moment became such a feature of the writings of James Boswell (1740 – 1795), especially in his study of the life of Samuel Johnson, that critics would later discuss the concept of Boswellian time for those instances where scenes run in the slowest of slow motion. By the early 19th century, the writers of the romantic movement sought out the power of nature; wilfully being washed in sensory experiences to achieve moments William Wordsworth described as "trances of thought and mountings of the mind."

In an act of late 18th century joy-riding Wordsworth stole a boat in the middle of a summer night on Ullswater. The incident forms a vivid section of his epic autobiographical poem, The Prelude.

"Within a rocky cave, its usual home.

Straight I unloosed her chain, and stepping in

Pushed from the shore. It was an act of stealth

And troubled pleasure....

Soon his feelings of guilt overtook him to the point the surrounding landscape appeared to be alive;

"a huge peak, black and huge,

As if with voluntary power instinct

Upreared its head. I struck and struck again,

And growing still in stature the grim shape

Towered up between me and the stars, and still,

For so it seemed, with purpose of its own

And measured motion like a living thing,

Strode after me."

Returning the boat, he couldn't shake the mental disturbance because;

"...huge and mighty forms, that do not live

Like living men, moved slowly through the mind

By day, and were a trouble to my dreams"

The Prelude was started in 1798 when Wordsworth was 28 but not published until 1850, a few weeks after his death.

The autobiographical Copsford (1948) appeared over a quarter of a century after Walter J C Murray spent a year in a leaking and remote house in Sussex. A military veteran depressed after an attempt to work as a journalist in London, he spent the year harvesting medicinal herbs. Eventually, the weather broke into his ramshackle home and drove him away. Far from depressed, he retreated having found the values that would shape his life. In Copsford's regular surges of energy the closeness to nature changes him; "A remarkable sense of freedom pervaded my being. Every common custom, every irksome convention, fell from me like broken fetters." [14]

Murray founded a school in Sussex and remained headmaster for 40 years. His love of nature informed his work, but he was much more middle-England than new age in his outlook. Copsford – however – still brings in a mysticism so close to William James' model of mystic experience that Murray's biographer has traced all its stages as they are teased out in the book, describing it as "the most beautiful account of a man connecting with nature" [15].

Wordsworth's epic autobiographical poem was published posthumously but an earlier (1805) version is also available, showing that he, like Walter J C

Murray and countless others consistently reviewed his work and considered its meaning. For many creative artists the experience of mystery has prompted thoughts that informed and guided their lives. For Murray the sense of the year in Copsford defining his values and the sudden encounters with natural forces being the cause is all the stronger because his initial vague plans were more concerned with escaping London and finding a means of making a living. Copsford does make it clear that the local schoolmistress who helped him as a 20-year-old is his wife by the time the book is written. It leaves out another defining event, the death at the age of 15 of their only child, a son. But Copsford is clear on the fact Murray's venture into nature with its obligation to respond to weather, the available daylight and the changing seasons brought a sense of connection that never left him.

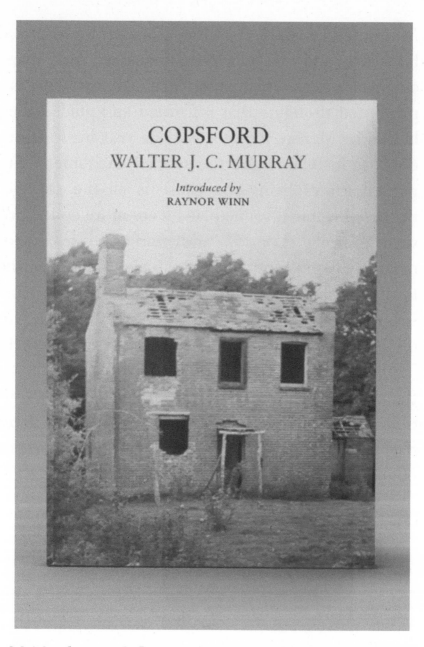

*2019 edition of Copsford, used by permission of Little Toller Books*

The writings of Wordsworth and Murray share a quality of mystic insight achieved partly through consistently reviewing the defining moments of mystery experienced as young men. Their maturity at the time of writing has allowed for them to focus on the most important aspects and employ their considerable literary skills to bring these moments to life for their readers.

Not long before Murray spent his year in the country Bertrand Russell's essay "Mysticism and Logic" argued "Mysticism is, in essence, little more than a certain intensity and depth of feeling in regard to what is believed about the universe… marriage with the world is not to be achieved by an ideal which shrinks from fact, or demands in advance that the world shall conform to its desires." Russell's words came at a time of a growing faith that technology and science would help man overcome all the major problems he faced. The unleashing of science and technology's most destructive powers in the First World War had a profound impact on that notion. The same pattern has repeated over the last century with technical advances and new inventions presenting themselves as some means by which the world will be completely changed. Cars, air travel and the growth of the internet have certainly changed our lives. The world filmed and photographed a century

61

ago seems quaint and quiet in many ways. But, through all these changes the tension between facts and feelings has been the site of our experience of mystery. As Russell points out, we can't shrink from fact and ignore truths. But it is those moments when feelings overwhelm us that can lead to the mystical process William James described and codified in 1902. For many people, encouraging those experiences remains central to their life choices and for a number of those seekers the process has also been the source of their work. Creative artists have celebrated this in many ways. William Blake, one of the greatest of all English mystical writers and artists noted in his work Heaven and Hell "If the doors of perception were cleansed, every thing would appear to man as it is: infinite." That conception has become a creed for many others, notably rock band The Doors who placed themselves firmly in the position of constantly seeking the mystic and channelling it when co-founder and keyboard player Ray Manzarek told Newsweek in 1967: "There are things you know about, and things you don't, the known and the unknown, and in between are the doors—that's us." The Doors, therefore, provide a clear example of a creative force in which audiences are openly invited to lose themselves in the abstract and mysterious. The lengthy instrumental passages in their best-known songs, like Riders on the Storm and Light my Fire are – in this context – the most meaningful parts of their music, representing those moments when band and audience experience insights together. This dynamic is central to lots of situations in which live music is experienced. Rave culture and its many offshoots have created a model of loud disorienting music with few, if any, words, attendant light shows and a permissiveness where drug use in concerned which have led some commentators to liken the whole experience to shamanic practice. The UK band Faithless repeat the phrase "This is my church" in their "God is a DJ" which talks about healing hurt and creating understanding and does so in a track widely used in the rave culture around the turn of the century. Crucially the track also refers in its second verse to the temporary nature of seeing into an ideal world with the line "for tonight, God is a DJ."

*Sister Bliss of Faithless*

Barry Lopez was a highly regarded nature writer working in a tradition within which bathing in the mysterious is a quest that brings meaning to life. His Autobiography, Horizon (2019) published shortly before his death, presents a summary of his observations. Notably, he sees himself as an artist who works in words, not a simply a writer. Having imagined himself early in his working life as "a courier" retrieving the messages of nature for his readers he subsequently expanded his view through personal experience. His experience includes seeing objects like rocks as possessing a life: "a stone, presented with…a certain kind of welcoming stillness, might reveal, easily and naturally, some part of its meaning." This notion also informs Robert MacFarlane's Underland which considers the perspective humans can achieve once they see the structures of the planet from under the ground and perceive the "deep time" on which the planet operates. In one chapter of Horizons, Lopez journeys into wilderness areas in search of what native Eskimo Alaskans call "earth and great weather." This is an experience he can't access other than in the wild. The local native language has one word that replaces the phrase "earth and great weather." The purpose of the one word is to encapsulate the importance of experiencing the environment during moments of intense weather and using this experience to achieve a perspective on the fact humans are simply part of the scene. Crucially, no more significant than the other parts. Horizon recounts a series of experiences in which Lopez visits extreme outposts inhabited by humans, in some cases temporarily as they venture out on archaeological digs. He repeatedly puts himself into situations in which nature will impact on him. He seeks out mystery and moments in which he encounters the mystic. Despite the book chronicling the work of a lifetime the encounters are always fleeting and what emerges consistently are growing opinions and insights. Lopez' work is best described as a polemic – an argument taking an opinionated stance and revealing this over the length of a book. In this case Horizon takes issue with western values and the notion of the planet as a resource to be raided by those in search of things to own and opportunities to make money. For Lopez the priorities in such action are destructive and misguided as they discount the values of other cultures. His moments of rapture lead to insights, particularly the notion "It has long seemed to me that what most of us are looking for is the opportunity to express, without embarrassment or judgement or retaliation, our capacity to love."

He argues that bringing about love and trust between all humans is the only hope for the planet. In a practical sense this is simply an argument in favour of a world in which varied cultures constantly attempt to understand and appreciate each other, accepting as they do that preserving our fragile world is a prize worth all the effort. The thought is contained in the title of Horizon and explained:

"when a *boundary* in the known world…becomes instead a beckoning *horizon*, the leading edge of a farther destination, then a world one has never known becomes an integral part of one's new universe." [Lopez' italics]. [17]

In one simple and pragmatic sense the choice to hurl yourself at a subject that overawes you and engage with the elements that challenge your thinking, in other words those bits that remain mysterious to you, can be the basis of enough work to sustain a career. I'm not being negatively critical this book is proof that I've chosen to make part of my living this way. So, whilst those people cited so far in this chapter made significant contributions to our understanding of mystery it's worth noting that for many of them it was – literally – the work of a lifetime when they did. This matters to our understanding of mystery because some the mysteries we encounter appear because people make conscious choices to ask questions, push boundaries and bring about situations where the unpredictable, including the forming of new questions, will arise naturally.

The work of academic Justin Gregg and his book If Nietzsche Were a Narwal (2022 US, 2023 UK) provides an intriguing example. Gregg's academic focus is on understanding animal intelligence, especially that of dolphins. He currently works as Adjunct Professor at St. Francis Xavier University, and a Senior Research Associate with the Dolphin Communication Project. His book asks profound questions about the value of cognitive intelligence as humans understand it, the core of his enquiry is expressed in his observation that "we truly are exceptional because of our complex cognition. But so what, are we better off for it?" [18]

As with many significant academic questions, and careers Gregg's choice of work, and his choice to present his arguments in a book give rise to so many questions that mysteries emerge along the way. The knowledge he presents and the arguments based on provable discoveries raise massive issues in fields like philosophy and morality. Crudely, he points out that the cognitive abilities of humans have at times been so destructive and dangerous that we might usefully learn from other life forms apparently less ambitious and narcissistic. Philosopher John Gray also noted that some "animals differ from humans…in lacking the sensation of selfhood. In this they are not altogether unfortunate. Self-awareness is as much a disability as a power." He qualifies this observation with discussions of cases in which "we are at our most skilful when we are least self-aware" [19] citing examples of playing the piano, working as a

68

craftsman and the case of Japanese archers being taught their accuracy will improve when they expend less effort thinking of the target.

Gregg and Gray highlight the way mystery makes sense to humans and is understood by us through our own peculiar intelligence. We are not unique as intelligent creatures – something Gregg knows first-hand from his work with dolphins – human intelligence comes with its own benefits and disadvantages. A beneficial way to use these abilities is to continue asking questions and learning so that our decision making isn't blinded by the disadvantages that come with our less attractive qualities, like greed and narcissism.

I'll take a brief authorial side-step here. I'd claim some understanding of many of the researchers and authors quoted in this work. Not because I share their knowledge or insights, but because I share something of their working methods whereby a collision of research, thought, the occasional moment of inspiration and the ongoing battle to present what we know in the best possible form of words, within some medium – book, live talk, podcast… - and within the demands of a market amounts to our "work". I'll also be honest in considering one place where my skills run out, and I need someone else's assistance. When I taught Professional Writing to undergraduates there were moments when their frank questions or their work gave me insights I'd otherwise be denied. One person who managed to test the limits of my skills several times is now credited as authoring this book "with" me. A few sessions into the course E K Knight asked me a question in class that left me thinking I didn't know the answer and would have to get back with it a couple of days later. It wasn't long before I realised the best way to get a good performance from E K was to explain the work to the whole class before taking a moment to ask, "how does that translate on your planet?" The question was pertinent given that E K's focus – then and now – was the creation of a dark fantasy world full of detail and nuance. I can tell you that in the context of a book about mystery this is an important detail because fiction authors, and especially those creating alternative realities, resemble academics in the way they collide with a massive subject, rich in the mysterious and then attack it in a way that explores the mysteries, raising more questions as it does.

Beyond which, E K will explain it far better than I can: I don't think about mystery. I just write it. Then I leave it to others to discover it. So when Neil approached me to co-author, I found myself at a loss for what, precisely, I was going to even say. What do *I* know about mystery?

And then it hit me.

What is fantasy but a mystery?

So, to answer my own question? Quite a lot, apparently, though perhaps not so traditionally.

I'm massively involved in my dark fantasy set in Region 8. So involved, in fact, I'm too busy being nose-deep reimagining the real world in a fantastical sense to pay much attention to it in reality.

I never considered it any sort of a challenge to slot the real world into the unreal world constructed of words. My main challenge was always, "Great, and now what do I do with it?"

Well, the bottom line of being an author – especially one who's presenting a world that's so much like ours but so much not – is to present you, the reader, with something you're clueless about in-regards-to what comes next.

My Region 8 is the city where everything happens. It's London. But it's not London, is it? So why is it Region 8? Why does everyone live there, not out there, in the smog that kills most and leaves the rest

71

so twisted, you're left wondering if the lucky ones had been the ones who'd died?

I want you to relate. And how can you not? Wake up on a particular winter's day and look out your window. You can't see fifty feet into the fog. Does your mind start to picture what's going to erupt from that mist? I do. And I want to share with you my workings.

In a dark fantasy where anything's possible… is a fog just a fog?

In my world, my book, the answer is no. No, it isn't. Of course it isn't. So now it's my job to extend my hand and lead you along this path of answers to all the questions that need to be asked, because here be dragons and what's erupting from that smog is going to be more than your local early-morning joggers or drunks stumbling back from a good night out.

Let me lure you into the mystery of my imaginings!

Stepping back to me, Neil, I think E K Knight has made a point on behalf of the most ambitious creative artists. The ability to inhabit an imagined realm is also an exploration of mystery. It's a route to discovery and an invitation to an audience to share the journey. I asked E K about the meaning of several things in the fictitious Region 8. I wasn't

72

surprised when I was told that some of the answers to my questions had emerged well after the work was started. One thing that strikes me is the simplicity of the observation "I don't think about mystery. I just write it." It's the kind of statement many creative artists make. A revelation that a world that appears fantastical to an audience is easily entered by the creative mind that first imagined it. It resonates with me because many creative artists I've admired have said similar things, revealing that their way of approaching their craft set them apart from the way others experienced the same thing. Rock guitarist Jimi Hendrix once discussed in an interview his intention to create music with less words and more meaning. On another occasion, discussing the dynamics of music he indicated he could "dig" Strauss and Wager. Apparently simple observations but hugely revealing of the way his approach to music was intuitive rather than intellectual.

Sometimes, creatively, we journey into the realms of our imagination without realising what we're discovering or why we're there. The common ground between this and other mysteries discussed here is - I think – the relationship between one individual and something so massive and detailed that it will reveal its mysterious secrets slowly, and only when the person is ready to understand them. We'll return to the role of art in finding a short-cut to presenting complicated ideas later, notably when graffiti artist CatNeil makes a brief appearance. Soon we'll discuss the importance of the small person/massive reality as we consider research made into the way people experience awe.

Few of the examples cited above come from people who argue the value of mystery for its own sake. For most, mystery is a route to a revelation and some insight they wish to share. The works quoted above are mainly commercial in the sense that some part of their making was always linked to an expectation of earning money. The trawl above is also a minute fraction of those cases when mystery has been experienced and some importance has been attached to that experience. It is also a survey largely focussed on cases in western culture and it is by no means representative of that culture. One point I think we can usefully make here is that the human brain has evolved the ability to experience and interpret the mysterious. Some see this as proof of a divinity creating us with the capacity to appreciate the divine. For others our abilities can be explained purely as a product of our own biological and social evolution, up to the point that our religions are the "byproduct" of our survival. The crucial point for me in closing this chapter is that the experience of mystery remains

74

central to our humanity, and we continue to give it value. This happens despite the changes our species has undergone in its choices about living and despite the distractions with which we choose to occupy ourselves. We are certainly hardwired to experience mystery, but we have choices about the importance we attach to such experiences. Crucially, we continue to express our interest in mystery by revisiting and reinventing the same processes. We seek out those overwhelming experiences in nature that unite Roger Ascham and Barry Lopez, or we create rituals. To an anthropologist studying cultures there are obvious similarities between the ghost dancing in the final days of the native Americans' conflict with the white settlers and the rave culture that afforded Faithless a hit single with God is a DJ. Most of us realize we can't force ourselves on demand into a moment of mystery. We can, however, make choices; hoping to bring about those instances when we release our sense of self far enough accept our own insignificance in the face of a greater reality. What we choose to do varies across cultures and across our history as humans. So too do the revelations we experience and the truths we choose to tell each other. What is beyond dispute is that mystery matters. It has mattered in the past and it continues to do so. I noted much earlier that: "Embracing the biggest mysteries is key to us understanding who we are and what purposes we can find in life." There is no bigger mystery than the thing identified in The Hitchhiker's Guide to the Galaxy as "The Ultimate Question." Most cultures have their own version of an answer. Many of these answers show marked similarities to each other in their creation myths. It is notable that more totalitarian regimes feel the need to exert their power in acts of destruction wreaked on the beliefs of those at odds with the totalitarian ideology. Camps calculated to demolish religious faith, the destruction of religious symbols and the development of substantial arguments designed to undermine the claims of religions all continue to be part of our world. They may achieve local success and short-term gains, but history has generally been harsh on the ambitions of dictators. The magnetic pull of mystery and the promise of deeper truths are not destroyed. Mystery matters because experiencing mystery is part of the human condition, and our history teaches us it always has been.

# CHAPTER THREE

# HARNESSING THE POWER OF MYSTERY

"We have traditionally struggled with the awe" – Avi Loeb: Extraterrestrial

Regardless of what mystery might have to teach us about The Ultimate Question it retains the power to enthral. It can intrude into lives, become a source of energy and power and – crucially – can take us to places that are otherwise hard to reach. This chapter considers some cases in which mystery has revealed more than anyone expected, teaching us lessons in the process.

There is no clear dividing line between those moments when some people claim to experience the divine and others simply see our psychology at work. One place where both are identified repeatedly is in dreams. The Ghost Dance was the result of a vision experienced within a coma. Some religious texts including the Bible contain accounts of insights imparted to people in dreams. Some religions revere the power of dreams to produce enlightenment. Scientific studies include several significant breakthroughs brought about through dreams. August Kekule's achievements place him amongst the most significant chemists of the 19$^{th}$ century, a founder of theoretical chemistry with significant discoveries to his name. By his own account the breakthrough that allowed him to appreciate the chemical structure of Benzene occurred when he lapsed into a doze in front of the fire after a gruelling attempt to solve the mystery. He reported a dream of a coiled serpent seizing its own tail and the image eventually allowed him to decipher the formula in which Benzene reveals itself as a six-membered ring of carbon atoms with alternating single and double bonds. Some dispute is attached to this story. If true, the dream probably occurred in 1862 but others suggest humorous stories about animal rings – including a vision of monkeys dancing around with linked hands – were in circulation in the scientific community at the time as a number of researchers attempted to understand the action of atoms within different elements.

Whatever the truth, an uncanny vision and the playful and abstract actions of a human mind eventually led to a major scientific breakthrough. There is no dispute about another dream-based revelation. The work that earned evolutionary biologist Margie Profet a MacArthur Fellowship in 1993 was based on her theory that women menstruate as a means of ridding their bodies of potentially harmful microbes attached to sperm. The thoughts prompting this paper allowed Profet to develop further ideas concerning the purpose of allergies. Her interest in the subject was first raised when as a young girl at school menstruation was explained to her and the prevailing wisdom of the late sixties presented it as a means of the body ridding itself of an unused egg and other tissues. It struck Margie as a wasteful way of nature solving the problem but it was an adult dream that focussed her attention on the idea that won her the fellowship. In her words: "I saw cartoon images of a woman's body, like the ones in the school film. The ovaries were pale yellow; the uterus was deep red. There were black triangles in the endometrium. Blood was coming out, taking the triangles with it. Then my cat meowed, wanting out—he was quite a nocturnal hunter. I woke up into this half-awake state and thought, 'The black things are pathogens—that's why!'"

Margie Profet is also famous for another reason. Her disappearance in 2005 and subsequent discovery after seven years in which she vanished so completely that those looking were unable to find any electronic record of her existence. An article covering her career and disappearance in Psychology Today considers testimony about her mental state from people who knew her closely and notes: "paranoia may have fuelled her genius. It may also explain her disappearance." Certainly, there is a parallel between what is known about Margie Profet's mental health and the notion of the human body expelling hostile elements which constantly threaten to attack it. The same relationship appears present in the dream she reports in which the black triangles represent a malevolent force. [1]

Another uncanny piece of dream research only revealed its full significance years after the event. Amongst allied prisoners of war held in Laufen Castle was Major Kenneth Hopkins. He planned a post-graduate dissertation after the war and began collecting the dreams of his fellow prisoners to provide the data set for his work. Hopkins died of a lung ailment in the camp, so the data set remained unstudied and unappreciated until the 21$^{st}$ century when it was discovered in the Wellcome Collection Medical Library. Gathered between 1940 and 1942 the dreams proved revealing when compared with recorded dreams of male students of the same period. The data shows most POWs dreaming less about common subjects in young men, like sex and aggression, and more about the concerns central to their war experience, like dead people and food. Hopkins could feel confident of reliable access to his sample because in the period the dreams were collected the war was going badly for the allies and Laufen Castle boasted a level of security that led to Germans to think it escape proof. Dreams of escape were relatively rare and those having such dreams were prone to express negative thoughts on the subject afterwards. There were a few who dreamt of escape and thought the experience positive. Significantly, there was a notable escape from the camp involving six men – one of whom was in the data set and had recorded an escape dream with positive feelings just before he managed to break out. [2]

Dreams collide the real and the surreal so successfully they have spawned a legacy of lore and literature devoted to their interpretation. Dreams matter as we consider mystery because they are an example of experiences we all share. An experience capable of ambushing us with mystery. Unusual events and uncanny feelings regularly appear in dreams, giving us some insight into the way all our minds work over problems in our lives. As we saw in the last chapter, our brains must work harder to disbelieve something than to believe it. They generally work harder, and for much longer to solve those problems that make us confused or uncomfortable. August Kekule and Margie Profet both had strong motivation to resolve scientific issues. Their conscious minds alone struggled to produce a clear solution.

For most of us there are moments of genuine mystery in life. Even those of us who love routines and security are faced regularly with difficult decisions. Such decisions present scenarios with the mystery of how closely we can imagine the outcome of some action we haven't yet committed ourselves to taking. Mystery in that sense is simply understanding that the result of our decision is unknown and therefore fits the simple definition of mystery as "anything that is kept secret or remains unexplained or unknown." When grappling with the unexplained or unknown requires significant amounts of mental energy, we can achieve those breakthroughs when we develop new knowledge, or a new sense of our capabilities.

Dmitri Shostakovich is one of the giants of 20$^{th}$ century classical music, but his standing wasn't easily achieved. A nervous and obsessive character who found it difficult to say no to people, he was torn for much of his working life between the creative impulses he felt and the very real threat to his livelihood, and life represented by the Soviet governments under which he lived. An early crisis occurred in the mid-1930's when the composer was denounced publicly in the state newspaper Pravda for presenting work that expressed little and failed to represent concerns consistent with Soviet values. For the rest of his life Shostakovich's work would be defined by genuine fears for his well-being, grounded in his knowledge that others were suffering and dying because of falling foul of the state. The problem he faced was one of presenting music of honesty in the situation. Some of the solutions were obvious and his fifth symphony was a triumph of conformity to accepted Soviet standards. Film music was less controversial and maintained an income, but the essential mystery Shostakovich spent much of his life exploring was how he could place himself inside the music when personal indulgences and anything too bourgeoise would lead to threats. The solutions to this hugely uncomfortable dilemma are central to the standing of his art today. One device used repeatedly was a musical motif, in effect a cryptogram based around the notes D, E flat, C, B natural which could be decoded to reveal a signature "DSCH." Shostakovich placed his signature in several works and composed pieces "for the desk drawer" intending to present them when the political climate allowed. Some of the most emotive and personal pieces he ever wrote were string quartets including the famous Eighth String Quartet of 1960. Apparently, a work commemorating the victims of fascism and war, produced in memory of the fire-bombing of Dresden in 1944, Shostakovich really intended the piece as a personal requiem for himself. Biographers and those close to him were aware he came close to suicide around the time of composing the quartet. The composer collapsed into tears on first hearing the work performed by the Borodin Quartet in his Moscow flat. He married for the third time in 1964 and lived until 1975 though the contradictions that stalked his life were always present and, whilst he avoided suicide, his later life was blighted by ill health which wasn't helped by his refusal to give up smoking or drinking Vodka. His best work negotiated the boundaries of political necessity and personal urges so well that Suzy Klein would later herald his: "masterpiece of grey areas and doublespeak." [3]

Shostakovich remains highly regarded because his best work is an invitation into the intensely personal. It expresses emotions and tells autobiographical stories. This is often achieved by bypassing the intellect to the point the most emotive passages can be regarded as the main point of a piece like his Eighth Quartet. Such abstract works exist in a place of emotional memory, their purpose being to share something way beyond information. The notion of "understanding" such a work is inseparable from the idea of sharing. In that sense they share something in common with the rave culture discussed earlier, the views of Jimi Hendrix and The Doors about their output which we also considered, and countless shamanistic and abstract sounds turned into musical works in all cultures.

Allowing mystery to exist solidly in our thinking as we resolve problems is one means of bringing about greater learning than we achieve if we simply seek facts and solutions to specific problems. In all the interviews, casual approaches after talks and other conversations about the paranormal I've had over the years one question has remained fairly constant. It's some version of "what is the answer to this mystery?" Note the definite articles, THE answer to THIS mystery. Clearly a radio or television interview often trades on some simple item of information as the bait to encourage an audience. My own view is different. In most cases of major areas of mystery, UFOs, ghosts, and the like, I'd say almost all the answers advanced are also explanations. UFOs, for example, are provably little understood natural phenomena, misidentifications of the mundane (like swarms of insects or planets located exactly where we'd expect to find them), hoaxes, individuals making eccentric interpretations of things others experience differently etc. So, in my humble opinion at least, grouping any such phenomena together in search of THE (singular) answer is misguided if you're attempting to locate the truth.

One thing I'd share about the years spent in search of answers in this area is the growing realization that one productive area of investigation is the study of those who find these fringe areas so fascinating. The following is a simplistic overview but useful if we are considering why mystery matters. Basically, over the decades since the second world war ufology in particular has followed a pattern within which the most spectacular claims all revolved around one or two cases popular at a given moment which, if proven to live up to the claims made about them,

86

would end for all time any debate about whether our planet was receiving visits from aliens. Alongside this pattern another body of research has gradually mined what is known about all the "conventional" explanations (hoaxes, misidentifications etc.) and taught us a lot that can be proven, certainly to the extent that it withstands peer review when offered for scientific publication. This is no small achievement given that UFO investigation in general is often a route to derailing an academic career. In my lifetime ufology has taught us a lot about natural phenomena, our own psychology, and other areas; generally, by producing a body of research work in which lessons learned by one study form further questions for the next researchers. Alongside this, the big cases touted as those that will finally convince the most dedicated sceptics have come and gone. There are still champions holding out for the realities of the Roswell case and a few other greatest hits but a casual internet search for a roll call of infamy taking in cases that were once amongst the greatest hits in this subject is easy. The 1995 alien autopsy film, MJ-12 documents or the Gulf Breeze sightings all found vocal champions and a great many words devoted to arguing their merits in various media. The presence of some genuine alien involvement in the tonnage of cases remains a possibility, but another truth emerges in the pattern above suggesting that our fascination with mysteries often reveals truths tangentially. The most popular mysteries of the present age produce patterns which resemble the strange personal experiences and unusual beliefs reported throughout history. It is often just the superficial details that change to suit a particular time, or place. History's most popular mysteries have sometimes fallen out of fashion. Belief in fairies or the willingness to attend public seances are significantly less popular than they once were. However, encountering enigmatic beings continues in reports of meetings with aliens and disembodied spirits still reach us, sometimes via mediums taking part in a ghost hunt. Some motifs of the stories remain strong even if the surface details change over time. Those visiting fairly realms centuries ago and those abducted by aliens more recently have brought back evidence – Joe Simonton's pancakes – for example, which usually lose their mystical properties when carefully investigated. Considered with hindsight some uncanny and mystery-based beliefs reveal themselves to have a pragmatic sense about them. A local superstition in the west country advocated a treatment for whooping cough in children in which the mother would "take her coughing child to three different parishes in one day." Apparently, an act of religious devotion in which the parent is pleading with God to intervene, this belief pre-dates motor cars so the resulting lengthy walk would, at least, offer some benefits of boosting the child's t-cell count and the operation of its immune system. [4]

In its simplest form mystery is that which is unknown or unexplained. We are capable of easily missing those places in our own thinking where we find an easy explanation and don't question it. A reminder, disbelieving something is a greater act of mental effort than accepting it. So, medical science has come a long way to understanding the role of the immune system in fighting infection and the belief about parish visiting, and whooping cough now makes sense in a secular way. For a long time, however, such medical superstitions – often with a religious element – made sense because they were seen to work so people took the easy route of believing the direct connection between God and health explained any improvement noticed. Elsewhere we gain from mystery when we use it to widen the questions we ask. Despite the widely taught and accepted views of human evolution it is notable that the fossil record supporting the investigation of that history is lacking over 90% of the definitive proof it needs. What we have are fragmentary glimpses and random finds to illustrate our most plausible theories in which mankind migrated from Africa, developing local adaptations in terms of body shape and skin colour as we did so. Much of the mystery of this story revolves around when and where the next significant fossil finds might emerge but in the early 1990s a controversial and major rethink of what we know was offered by Misia Landau. Her book Narratives of Human Evolution compared the research by the likes of Charles Darwin that had fuelled evolutionary theory with theories of myth and story-telling. Her argument, crudely, being that the classic hero's journey that forms the template to the present day for the most widely consumed stories, like those in Hollywood movies, has been adopted by evolutionary theorists to the point we blindly accept notions of our own evolutionary history being a version of that classic quest. The quest is typically one in which a brave individual sets out on a journey, is gifted power or an object of power from some mysterious force and overcomes odds to finally achieve a goal. [5] Landau's work didn't find favour with those who rely on the fossil record, but it is one example of another valuable aspect of mystery. In the many areas of human understanding in which we're still trying to find definitive truths, sometimes simply asking open-ended questions, and bringing in useful thinking from some other source is the most creative and enlightening thing we can do. When mysteries challenge our ability to make sense, they can also be empowering in teaching us about our creative capabilities.

When ideas oppose each-other they have the potential to produce the dialectic (basically a collision between opposing points of view) which has the power to bring any investigation closer to the truth. Some major new ideas intruding on areas of investigation may be unwelcome; Misia Landau's opinions certainly drew some hostile responses when they first appeared. However, the role of mystery in forcing people to think critically is easy to overlook. Ironically, many of the best- selling and most popular media works on mystery achieve their status partly through presenting specific solutions they know will appeal to their audiences. Crudely, the promise mystery but plan to present answers. The award winning and long-established podcast series, Skeptoid, typically devotes individual episodes to debunking myths and exploring claims of conspiracy or the paranormal. The series unleashed more minutes of content and some of its most scathing demolitions on the perennially popular television series Ancient Aliens. Skeptoid used critical thinking and verified historical records to demonstrate that several artefacts believed to betray the visits of alien races to the Earth were likely nothing of the sort, and some of the most estimable achievements of our ancestors owed everything to their ingenuity and nothing to technically superior visitors from other planets. Towards the end of the third episode devoted to the searing dissection of the disinformation on offer Skeptoid charged: "Ancient Aliens is, at its core, a slap in the face to the ingenuity of the human race. It charges that humans were not smart enough or industrious enough to build great works and great art, and therefore the explanation for the existence of these things must be alien intervention." [6] Popular as it is, Skeptoid is unlikely ever to approach the levels of popularity enjoyed by shows like Ancient Aliens or UFO Hunters. Skeptoid's statement above does – however - highlight a key element of the way we process mystery and often devalue its potential. The charge of slapping the human race in its collective face argues that confirmation bias rather than critical thinking drives much of our understanding of the mysterious. Put simply, we interpret mysteries in line with our current beliefs and we are often encouraged to do so when a documentary, book or other source promises us "the truth." It is easier to believe something than to put in the mental effort to disbelieve and question it. The media industry has sold us stories of mystery for centuries on this basis. There is no trustable figure isolating the financial value of the mysterious to the media. For many years the word "infotainment" was widely used to describe a genre in which information was presented successfully as true but often skewed so much to the needs of an audience that infotainment, a term suggesting the resulting content was at least halfway to entertainment, seemed an appropriate label. Whatever the actual percentages of factual truth in much of this content, defining it as infotainment is a description that makes clear it is more about presenting one version of a story than encouraging an audience to reason their way through a series of strange events. Ironically, the critical thinking encouraged by the likes of Skeptoid is a much more effective route to getting the most value out of mystery in your own life. Wrestling with the unexplainable and reasoning your way to an answer, with or without help, is the way to engage the bulk of your thinking and gain those moments in your own when the mysterious makes you feel more alive and involved. Skeptoid give succinct demonstrations of the difference between confirmation bias and the value of good old-fashioned critical thinking with their regular "pop quiz" episodes within which listeners are challenged to answer questions relating to the mysterious. The answers often reveal that a combination of common sense and the odd uncanny truth goes a long way to explaining the strangest things we experience. For example, the smaller doors in mediaeval houses have often been explained away as evidence of just how short people were at that time. Medieval people were certainly shorter on average than we are, but nowhere near as short as the doors in their surviving houses suggest. Their doors were typically smaller to reduce drafts, a major problem in the days before centralised heating systems or effective portable heaters. [7]

We know about medieval doors in the same way we know the genuine answers to many perplexing questions, because research and a body of evidence has been built-up to tell us the answer to a question. There is satisfaction in grappling with a problem to the point that it reveals a solution. Satisfaction too when the answer is also a lesson of some kind, even if it only points out our own folly in believing a common misconception. Mystery, matters in these circumstances partly because it focusses the question into some form of How? Why? What? It also matters because it presents the opportunity to immerse ourselves in the unresolved and sometimes uncomfortable feelings and work our way out again. As with the question in the first chapter revolving

94

around answering The Ultimate Question, attempting to solve a major problem often presents us with a useful experience. The world is awash with easy answers and sometimes the simple solution of finding them is too tempting. Easy answers have their place. Few people want to experiment with options when the owners-manual of a car presents a helpful diagram explaining how to reset the dashboard clock to summertime. But bigger problems, like those relating to career, relationships and other life choices aren't well served with simple answers – however tempting they may seem to be. Many people later in life come to value what was gained in struggling to reach answers. These problems don't present obvious mysteries in the way the existence of a God might present them. However, they often mimic such mysteries, certainly in the way our minds gravitate to "if only…" ideas about simple answers, particularly those simple answers that tempt us into thoughts of knowing the outcome of some choice before we make it. We can experience the mysterious in such moments because we experience a sense of our own lack of power in the face of a great problem, even if the problem is only great to us. Mankind's sense of impotence may have been central to the development of our greatest religious stories. It is certainly central to the lasting power of these stories. On a very personal level we often tell our own scaled down versions of this tale of being confronted with great challenges and valuing our own ingenuity to achieve the outcome we want. We tell these tales when we explain our choices in careers, relationships, and other major life decisions. The value of these stories to us depends to a great extent on our ability to remain within those moments of discomfort and confusion, and to experience the mystery of not knowing the outcome. Solving the mundane mysteries of day-to-day life contributes massively to the sense of who we are and how we live. It is no accident that talking therapies often employ a strategy within which the therapist may reflect back some of the things said by a client. There are many reasons for this, linked to gradually teasing out truths and making significant changes in life. But in one simple sense there is value in this reflecting because it brings focus to unravelling the hardest problems we face. The goal is understanding and personal growth. For many of us similar revelations come randomly, sometimes after years of processing the most problematical aspects of our lives. When I taught Professional Writing students one of the toughest mysteries they faced was to identify and express any sense of who they were and what made their creative talents unique. This mattered in a very practical sense because the ability to explain your own particular gifts is central to getting the right employment, especially as a new graduate when the balance between what you say you can do and what you can prove you have already done puts your potential employer in a very powerful position. We often discussed this issue in class and effective strategies were always part of the these discussions. However, during the period I did this work I had an uncanny experience which eventually became a story I told the students.

Oddly, it seemed very inconsequential at the time. In a pub before a football match, I met the usual crowd of fellow travellers who randomly gather on such occasions. We're a down to earth group. We follow the fortunes of Carlisle United, and we are usually away supporters at whichever game we attend, being members of the "London Branch" of exiles. For anyone outside the UK reading this, all you need to know is that this is grassroots support of a moderately successful club undertaken by people you'd never describe as glory hunters. Just about the only thing that unites this very varied bunch is our mutual love of our club. Consequently, much of the pre-match banter, especially over a beer or two, is light-hearted as we gather in venues we see once a year. One fellow traveller that day calmly informed me that my way of making a living "talking to groups of people and then sitting at home to think things up" was his idea of Hell. I didn't think too deeply about the reply in which I said something like "…you don't get it. I've suffered from ideas my whole life and all I've done jobwise is land myself in situations where that affliction is useful." We had a laugh, decided I'd be equally uncomfortable if I found myself in my friend's job (train driving) and went off to watch a game that hasn't lasted anywhere near as well in my memory as that conversation. The reason the conversation has stayed with me is that soon after leaving the game I found myself turning it over in my mind and suddenly realized it was probably the most incisive and truthful way I could explain a career based on professional creativity. More significantly, that honest and unassuming answer simply felt more accurate than the tonnage of carefully crafted arguments I've submitted over the years as I've chased deals to get my ideas published and performed. Having been married to a psychotherapist for decades I have some insight into the origins of my "affliction," and I have also become fairly effective at managing it. So, the remark about landing myself in situations where this is useful did indeed feel honest because I could easily recall many different times in which I'd instinctively put myself in a position of having to deliver some creative work. By contrast, thinking about the arguments that often went along with book submissions I could feel they held some truth but not the whole truth. Getting to the simple point of what had driven the bulk of my working life, was far from simple. It was, however, the end of a lengthy set of collisions with something mysterious as I'd tried to put into words, and feelings exactly what it was that made my experience my own.

For many people in countless ways the same moments of revelation emerge to finally put into focus some lifelong quest for personal understanding. You don't need a therapist to do this, but in some cases, they might offer the most helpful route. Whatever your route to a truth that makes logical sense and feels honest emotionally, it's generally an example of the value of pondering on mystery. We may be used to understanding mystery as something that belongs in those areas of life we label as "the mysterious" (i.e., the realm of the paranormal, conspiracies, missing persons and unsolved criminal acts) but we experience most mystery in our own lives with the kind of uncanny problems that gnaw away at us over a long time.

It's no accident that the methods of problem solving we value the most often arise from struggling with the areas of understanding we find hardest to define. The whole point of dialectic which we discussed earlier is to develop a process of knocking away at opposing arguments until what remains is the closest to truth it is possible to reach. No system of demystifying the unknown is perfect, but dialectic remains as the bedrock for advancing human understanding. Peer reviewed academic publishing continues to respect it. At its best, dialectic forces us to engage long and hard with the things we truly struggle to understand and challenges us all the way to an answer. If the answer in these circumstances isn't satisfying it can still be valuable. Firstly, because we know it's as good an answer as we can get and secondly because it's a route to more and better questions. Another model of understanding knowledge under-pins more mundane areas of academic work, notably the way we understand learning and the way inspection regimes in schools and colleges identify it. Bloom's Taxonomy developed between 1949 and 1953. Named after Benjamin Bloom, who chaired the whole process the taxonomy was outlined in publications including Handbook I: Cognitive (1956) and Handbook 2: Affective (1964). It is most highly valued in places like colleges that see training as a substantial part of the role they play. Like any system of understanding knowledge that aims to be definitive Bloom's Taxonomy has drawn fierce criticism and spawned alternatives. It is useful here in terms of looking at the difficulty of mapping what we know and how it relates to the things we find hardest to understand. The original taxonomy in 1956 identified synthesis (in which we create a new pattern or knowledge by blending diverse sources) as the second highest form of knowledge, surpassed only by evaluation (or the ability to understand what we have done). More recent revisions have argued for the swapping of these two with synthesis, as an act of doing and achieving, being a more significant expression of knowledge. The affective, or emotional taxonomy has proven harder to resolve. Bloom's original hierarchy in 1964 placed characterizing (or the ability to build abstract knowledge) at the pinnacle of this list. The arguments in this second domain convinced fewer people and the subjectivity of this area means no definitive list has emerged. But Bloom's continues to matter because it drove a debate that produced contrasting ideas. One result of the controversy is a general agreement that we identify the highest forms of knowledge in those areas in which we strive to understand the most mysterious and elusive ideas, and those times when we aim for responses that simply feel right. When these elements are aligned, we express our learning in the most profound ways.

An interesting case that demonstrates some of Bloom's ideas in action also confronts another of humanity's longest-lasting mysteries. University lecturer Vic Tandy spent some of his early career employed in the labs of a medical equipment company. Working in a room widely believed to be haunted he felt the classic reaction reported by others when confronted with a ghostly presence. Tandy felt cold but noticed he was sweating and sensed a presence in the room when he was clearly alone. Eventually he saw a ghostly shape in his peripheral vision. When he looked directly at it, the shape vanished. A chance event sparked an investigation that led, eventually, to a paper accepted for publication. When polishing his fencing sword soon after his ghostly encounter, Tandy noticed it vibrating when clamped in a vice and found himself speculating on the cause of the vibration being infrasound; slow moving soundwaves so low in frequency as to be inaudible to humans. An investigation of infrasound waves in the lab where Tandy had his ghostly experiences showed they were in their highest concentration next to his desk. Tandy was able to link the frequency – 19 Hz – at which infrasound waves have their highest emotional impact on humans to the conditions in his lab and publish a joint paper discussing his findings. The ghostly shape he saw was – in Tandy's analysis – best explained as the brief result of an interaction between a standing wave in the lab and water vapour in the air. One suggestion from the research was that certain locations, believed haunted, shared physical characteristics with Tandy's lab and might – therefore – be expected to produce similar phenomena. The significance of the paper was the new ground broken in attaching known science about the impact of sound waves to an area of human experience and belief. The argument was an act of synthesis, drawing together sciences that were seldom combined by academics. Synthesizing elements from, apparently unrelated areas of his life started Vic Tandy's investigation and a crucial element in developing the understanding of what was going on was an emotional, almost subjective component in which he was able to match his own sensitive response to the first strange incident with a scientific fact about the impact of a particular infrasound frequency on humans. Simply, Tandy was able to argue that the phenomena he observed both effected and affected people. Given the cold feelings that marked the start of his encounter it is ironic that he discovered the source of the 19 Hz standing wave discovered in his lab was a cooling fan. [8]

In the previous chapter we considered the extent to which our religions and other attempts to make sense of The Ultimate Question may be the side effect of the evolution of our species. We may be hard-wired to speculate on our own existence. We are certainly hard-wired to solve problems. Our brains, sensory apparatus, and the cultures we have constructed throughout our history all remind us of this. Gathering appropriate information, acting on it and learning from mistakes allowed humans to become the planet's dominant species. The first problems solved were those of survival. Hunter gathering humans had to resolve problems of managing time, space and distance to ensure their efforts in feeding and clothing themselves were achievable without exhaustion or endangering their safety. Agricultural humans were challenged more by issues of the yearly cycle of weather, the availability of water and appropriate land, and by managing a community to share the work. Our history as a species is partly one of increasingly complex problems solved in ways that made sense at the time. The archaeological record and cultural works left behind can provide clear snapshots of how we understood the pressing issues of a particular time. As an example, there is no doubt that Gilbert White's The Natural History of Selborne (1789) is a classic work of nature study. Written by a curate who recorded the natural world around him, the work is constructed of correspondence sent to others with an interest in flora and fauna. It is made up mainly of White's observations. Issues like bird migration and the behaviour of particular animals presented mysteries we have now largely solved but White's work is also notable for a tone that betrays his social class and several assumptions of the time which show the thinking as he attempts to answer the questions that taxed him. Sometimes he sees fit to cite poets like John Milton in seeking to understand the character of a particular bird. Elsewhere understanding is reached with methods we would find unacceptable today. When Honey Buzzards nest in the parish "a bold boy" is dispatched to climb to the nest and retrieve the solitary egg, which reveals a lot about the embryo contained. The hen bird is described in detail, after she has been shot and dissected. Elsewhere White's prose can present a world in which the polite society of his day is revealed even as he discusses the natural world; "I was much entertained last summer with a tame bat, which would take flies out of a person's hand. If you gave it anything to eat, it brought its wings round before the mouth, hovering and hiding its head in the manner of birds of prey when they feed. The adroitness it showed in shearing off the wings of the flies, which were always rejected, was worthy of observation, and pleased me much. Insects seem to be most acceptable, though it did not refuse raw flesh when offered: so that the notion that bats go down chimneys and gnaw men's bacon, seems no improbable story. While I amused myself with this wonderful quadruped, I saw it several times confute the vulgar opinion, that bats when down on a flat surface cannot get on the wing again, by rising with great ease from the floor. It ran, I observed, with more dispatch than I was aware of; but in a most ridiculous and grotesque manner." [9] Vivid passages like these are one reason Gilbert White is still read and appreciated today. They remind us that the wisdom and assumptions of one age will eventually change. What remains completely constant from White's writing to the present generation of nature writers is the work of peeling away layers to make sense of what is studied and the feeling that those observing have a personal sense of involvement as their work begins to provide answers. White is amused and willing to share with his society. Robert MacFarlane's observations in Underland are more understated and akin to present day reportage journalism. Both writers, however, would probably recognise a kinship with each other. More significantly from the perspective of understanding the value of mystery in our lives both writers may well bond over a common experience of being overwhelmed and in awe of the natural world they explore. Despite centuries of attempting to describe and contain the mysteries of nature it is notable that one recent study made international news simply because it reinforced an experience that humans have been describing since our written and artistic records began. Based at the University of California in San Francisco Virginia Sturm, associate professor of neurology and of psychiatry and behavioural sciences and the John Douglas French Alzheimer's Foundation Endowed Professor in the UCSF Weill Institute for Neurosciences reported on research in which healthy, older, adults took 15 minute "awe walks" at least once a week. Her partner in the research – psychologist Dr. Dacher Keltner – described the "awe" under scrutiny in the study as; "…a positive emotion triggered by awareness of something vastly larger than the self and not immediately understandable—such as nature, art, music, or being caught up in a collective act such as a ceremony, concert or political march." The evidence of improvement in mood and sense of well-being was blatant for those taking the walks and the newsworthiness of the study was helped greatly because the subjects were requested to take selfies at the start, middle and end of their walks. The selfies spoke for themselves, mainly because they exhibited a pattern in which the subjects of the selfies made sure they appeared less and the surroundings appeared more as their walks progressed. A control group involved in the study included several people who suspected the purpose of the research was to measure the benefits of exercise and some of these people decided to take more walks. Their level of benefit was less than the awe walkers. Sturm's major areas of expertise include research into Alzheimer's Disease and the awe walk study had been conceived as something akin to academic light relief. But its clear findings and simple message suggested the researchers had stumbled on something both timeless and massively important to who we are. As quoted in Medical Xpress Sturm noted; "One of the key features of awe is that it promotes what we call 'small self,' a healthy sense of proportion between your own self and the bigger picture of the world around you." [10] Keltner's subsequent book on the subject was highly positive on the value of experiencing awe, the subtitle stating "The New Science of Everyday Wonder and How It Can Transform Your Life. Keltner's "new science" drew on existing knowledge but employed recent studies to focus on conclusions with a very old school feel. For example, "it is hard to imagine a single thing you can do that is better for your body and mind than finding awe outdoors....Our bodies respond to healthy doses of awe-inspiring nature like we respond to a delicious and nutritious meal, a good sleep, a quenching drink of water...we feel nourished, strengthened, empowered and alive."[11]

There is a danger that we interpret the past in the light of our present attitudes. We can be certain that cave art and other expressions of early man's creativity were appreciated by the communities of the time. How far – for example – depictions of running wild animals were attempts to control real wildlife and bring luck on a hunt is less clear. One constant in most of what we know about our relationship with the natural world is that some element of "small self" has often been present as we represented and attempted to engage with our natural environment. We have often sought the same small self in the way we experience and share events in stories. Our encounters with the present stars of paranormal experiences, like aliens, have some shared elements with age old stories of encounters with nature spirits and in those cases individual humans are often left bemused and overwhelmed as

109

they are reminded of their limitations. On the most pragmatic level jobs in which people engage with the public often return the highest levels of job satisfaction in surveys. The notion of all jobs having an innate dignity and intelligence and of work being the primary impulse of human beings fuelled the book Working (1974) edited by Louis "Studs" Terkel. The subtitle of the work "People Talk About What They Do All Day and How They Feel About What They Do" is key to his belief that everyone has the capacity to employ their intelligence and find meaning in what they do.

*Louis "Studs" Terkel*

[12] To explore this point Terkel divides his work into themed chapters (called books) and links the people reporting back in terms of some common qualities in what they do rather than the traditional social status of a job. In the second book one theme explored is how people communicate effectively when their job depends upon this skill. He links people across varied careers and social standing including a hotel switchboard operator, a professor of communications, an airline reservationist and a sex worker. Much of the value people have found in Terkel's work over the years comes in those insightful moments when his subjects explain how they manage their jobs and gain a sense of satisfaction. Unsurprisingly, the switchboard operator in the hotel does listen in on calls, especially when she finds herself on a quiet nightshift. Most of us have held shared insights about our work with others.

*Switchboard operators before cell phones were a thing!*

A constant theme of such exchanges is discussing those moments when our working lives have tested us, and we have responded by finding some quality in ourselves. One lesson from such experiences is often that the real value of any such moment is the way it builds us as individuals. It is no accident that the best plumbers or nurses – for example – are empathic people who value their work partly for the experience of being able to benefit others. Superficially there may appear to be a long distance between a plumber solving a problem on an emergency call out and a scientist like Vic Tandy applying his knowledge and skills to proving a theory. Considered from the highly pragmatic point of view that characterises the work of Studs Terkel those experiences are very similar because they are about solving problems and finding some value in the sense of small self. Considered from Benjamin Bloom's taxonomy they are examples of synthesis, where skills training works best because it is combined with personal qualities. None of the people profiled in the book Working, or a present- day emergency call out plumber are experiencing themselves as a small self in the sense of the awe walkers reported on by Virginia Sturm. They, and we, however, can find the most meaningful moments in the times when the challenge we face is more than a simple practical problem like a leaking tap or connecting a phone call. The sense of connecting with others and being part of something bigger informs a lot of our day-to-day experience. We often don't name it in that way or even admit it but the common sense that leads some people to work in which they can constantly connect, and express empathy is also essential for health. Studies that look at the alternatives demonstrate this point. Several research projects have made it clear that the mental damage done by a job you hate easily equals that wreaked by unemployment. One University of Manchester study noted; "a clear pattern of the highest levels of chronic stress for adults who moved into poor quality work, higher than those adults who remained unemployed. Adults who found a good quality job had the lowest levels of biomarkers." This study sampled 1000 individuals, focussing particularly on the employment practices that denied individuals much chance to express themselves or find emotional connection to their work. [13] "Good quality" jobs in the context of this study are not about high salaries and prodigious perks. Despite the complexities of our relationship with work there remain some simple elements that go a long way to explaining the links between the small self, the way we behave at work and the studies highlighting the danger to our health of working environments that ignore our basic human needs. We feel, and function, better when our working environment helps us to produce the positive

115

chemicals that enhance our well- being – like dopamine, oxytocin and serotonin. Those situations in which we find ourselves engrossed, engaged, motivated and hopeful are generally those which bring about the best production of these essential and naturally occurring chemicals. One consistent feature of the examples in this chapter is that dynamic in which individuals find themselves in a position likely to bring about the best conditions for production of the more positive brain chemicals. Humanity evolved as a species surrounded by forces beyond our control, surviving in an environment that best rewarded us when we respected it and felt a connection. Maintaining this connection and bonding with others has been hard-wired in us to the point it benefits our health.

As we saw at the outset, mystery is a concept so complex that it has multiple definitions in our dictionaries. All forms of mystery, from a detective novel to a divinity trying to reach us, puzzle us and require us to respond. Mystery can put us in our place and remind us of our limitations. In the face of mystery, we are a smaller self, at least, and often the same small self we saw discussed by Virginia Sturm and Dacher Keltner.

Mystery is key to us developing significant new knowledge and key to those experiences that shape us and give a sense of direction. "Direction," however, is a negotiable concept. Its meaning from culture-to-culture changes considerably. The implied meaning of your direction in western cultures is often to do with a strategy for career advancement, perhaps through gaining qualifications and making sacrifices to achieve gains. Someone gaining a PhD in Molecular Genetics and then forsaking a burgeoning science career to live as a monk might appear to lack direction. Matthieu Ricard, who did just that, achieved world-wide fame for a completely different reason. A study into the activities in human brains carried out over 12 years at the University of Wisconsin identified Ricard as the world's happiest person. The evidence for the claim came from the monitoring of his brain activity. Predictably, Ricard believes the title to be a hyped-up media notion. He is in a good position to know because he combines his prolonged meditation practices and veganism with involvement in research (particularly into the benefits of meditation), photography and taking part in high profile gatherings; up to attending the World Economic Forum in Davos. He's happy to use the tools of modern life, an Apple Mac – for example – helps enormously when he needs to send his photographs around the world. But he can happily spend an entire day meditating without feeling bored, and that is proven by the results produced when the University of Wisconsin study wired electrodes to his head and produced a record of his brain activity.

This short chapter set out to explore mystery's power to enthral. It's ability to intrude into lives, become a source of energy and power in itself and – crucially – take us to places that are otherwise hard to reach. Regardless of your religious persuasion mystery is a reminder of our relative insignificance, a reminder too that we achieve the most when we strive to be part of something bigger. Mystery can produce empathy in us and a sense of connection. It challenges us to respond, sometimes by thinking, sometimes by being aware. There is no single way we can all take advantage of the aspects of mystery covered in this chapter, but we can all benefit from what engaging with mystery has to offer us. This matters now, probably, more than ever in our history because the experience of mystery has never been more under threat. The dedication demonstrated by Matthieu Ricard is likely at a level many of us would find daunting, But his ability to inhabit a mystic – in his case – meditative realm and still deal effectively with demanding areas of the real world is instructive because he is provably happier and more fulfilled than many of us believe possible. [14]

A more down to earth example and a fitting way to conclude this chapter involves considering the opinions of another influential thinker, novelist Kurt Vonnegut. In an interview promoting one of his final books Vonnegut discussed how his choices about buying an envelope contrasted with his wife's way of tackling the same problem, the key difference being the delight he could take in the unknown and the unexpected. "'Oh,' she says, 'well, you're not a poor man. You know, why don't you go online and buy a hundred envelopes and put them in the closet?' And so I pretend not to hear her. And go out to get an envelope because I'm going to have a hell of a good time in the process of buying one envelope. I meet a lot of people. And see some great looking babies. And a fire engine goes by. And I give them the thumbs up. And I'll ask a woman what kind of dog that is. And, and I don't know. The moral of the story is - we're here on Earth to fart around. And, of course, the computers will do us out of that. And what the computer people don't realize, or they don't care, is we're dancing animals. You know, we love to move around. And it's like we're not supposed to dance at all anymore." [15]

# CHAPTER FOUR

# THE WAR AGAINST MYSTERY

"The possession of knowledge does not kill the sense of wonder and mystery. There is always more mystery." Anais Nin

Nobody has declared war on mystery. If they had it might have been easier to map out some of the arguments in this book because a declaration of war would have exposed those to whom mystery is a threat. It might also have obliged them to identify mystery as an enemy and explain where mystery presented them with a legitimate target. The "war" in this chapter exists somewhere between the "War on Drugs" waged by some politicians and law enforcers and the general "war" incited by groups like advertisers when they try to associate any notion of military power with their mission to achieve an aim. In the case of the war on drugs the phrase and central ideas are most closely associated with the early years of the presidency of George W Bush. In a defining statement on his policy, he said; "Drug abuse threatens everything, everything that is best about our country...It breaks the bond between parent and child. It turns productive citizens into addicts. It transforms schools into places of violence and chaos. It makes playgrounds into crime scenes. It supports gangs at home." Bush also suggested anyone using recreational drugs was supporting global terror – since some of the earnings from the trade have fuelled activities defined as terrorism by western governments. Bush presented his war as a crusade to uphold a set of conservative values in which communities remained united, citizens were healthy and productive and the country housing these people maintained its moral code and sense of unity. Ironically, his phrase subsequently became the name of a successful rock band for whom the very vagueness of the phrase, up to and including seeing it as ironic, had a value. As their vocalist and songwriter - Adam Granduciel – explained it "My friend Julian and I came up with [the name] a few years ago over a couple bottles of red wine and a few typewriters…it just came out and we were like 'hey, good band name' so eventually…I used it…I think we made the right choice. I always felt though that it was the kind of name I could record all sorts of different music under without any sort of predictability inherent in the name." [1]

So, George W Bush's "war" was a targeted campaign against the impact and influence of drugs, intended to rally conservative opinion and strengthen the shared values of many Americans. Another group of Americans found commercial success and critical respect without ever wanting to define their relationship with the phrase, which they simply felt was a good name for their band.

Mystery as a concept is vague enough to demand multiple definitions and in-that-sense clearly resembles the drugs against which the Bush administration declared war. This is so largely because Bush's war on drugs was usually couched in general notions that roped in ideas of how society should behave, the threats to everyone if things went wrong and the lingering menace of those who stood to gain if the war failed. There are no clinical definitions of Class A mysteries but clearly there is a difference in degree between the mystery of where we all fit in the great cosmic conundrum and where, exactly, that pungent smell wafting down your street is coming from. But in just the same way as the generality of drugs and drug culture was a threat to values many saw as quintessentially American the generality of mystery is a threat to many areas of day-to-day life which gain most when we behave in predictable ways.

In this regard, those working to marginalize the mysterious do unite to wage something akin to a war. They do so because their lives are better if mystery is constantly eradicated and driven out. It's a concept we encounter frequently in other places. Notably in advertising when we are challenged to believe in our own power to join a shared crusade. For years advertisers have incited gardeners to join the "war on weeds." So much so that the phrase and the notion aren't challenged when they make frequent appearances in adverts or other promotion. The reasons gardeners may want to join the war are usually obvious. So, the call to action from those catering to the market relies on us trusting their knowledge and taking advice like: "HOW TO WIN THE WAR ON WEEDS. If you let weeds gain a foothold, you'll have trouble for months and even years to come, but to gain control and win the war against weeds you will need to get to know your enemy. The commonest weeds in your garden are not necessarily the ones you should worry about most. These are generally annuals that seed themselves..." [2] This article – posted online by an out-of-town shopping experience on the edge of London catering to gardeners and offering café facilities went on to profile a range of weeds in a "know your enemy" section.

The mysterious and vague are a threat to those who seek to sell us specific solutions to problems; or guide us through an experience towards a conclusion that suits them. It makes sense to solve a problem by buying or hiring the solution, like weed killer. Similarly, it makes sense to search out things you might want – like information. Increasingly these experiences are online and the providers managing us towards their calls to action employ marketing techniques known and used for years. The cost we can pay for this was succinctly expressed in a best-selling book marketed to those in business aspiring to be leaders. "In our pursuit to advance, we have, without intending to, built a world that is making it harder and harder for us to cooperate...Feelings of isolation and high stress have fuelled industries that are profiting from the search for happiness...The biggest thing the self-help industry seems to have helped is itself." [3] Simply, the further we are

125

funnelled into discreet communities the more distant we feel from each other as a species. The end results are increased anxiety and widespread mental health problems which tipped into meltdown proportions for many caring agencies once the Covid 19 pandemic took hold. At the other end of the spectrum, we have sought to eradicate a set of emotional responses central to our humanity, like ennui. It seems harder than it used to be – for example – to set out for a walk and simply be overtaken by an emotional response to the play of sunlight on nearby trees. The temptation to snap the moment on a phone and share it might be the automatic thought that follows you noticing the autumn leaves reflecting the setting sun. Granted, the subjects in Virginia Sturm's study gradually pictured themselves as a less significant element of the selfie as their awe walks progressed but they had been instructed to walk for enough time to let their surroundings work on them. Their instructions were designed to move them away from thoughts of being constantly in contact with their online community.

The countless online operations that make money when they snag our attention benefit from a world in which we experience ourselves as belonging to like-minded groups with shared interests. The business terminology generated in the internet age values "eyeballs" and to a lesser extent, ears as their equivalent of footfall. In the present century the concept of a "reality-based community" has – for many – become an identifier of a community of the mis-guided. The phrase goes back to a reported conversation between New York Times journalist Ron Suskind and an anonymous aide to George W Bush. "The aide said that guys like me were 'in what we call the reality-based community,' which he defined as people who 'believe that solutions emerge from your judicious study of discernible reality.' I nodded and murmured something about enlightenment principles and empiricism. He cut me off. 'That's not the way the world really works anymore,' he continued." [4] By which he meant that the new leaders saw the "reality-based community" as a bunch of people to be derided, perhaps even pitied. As with the notion of a war on drugs, there are others since this time who have taken the derisory term and chosen to proudly out themselves as believers in facts and solving problems from the study of reality. But, that conversation early this century marks a significant moment in the travel of a world more focussed on finding an identity around shared values and views than in fact. One frustrating truth for those in the USA concerned about climate change is that many of a strong religious persuasion don't perceive a problem. Far from it, some of them see the projected heating of the world as the fulfilment of a biblical prophecy and remain unconcerned because if the wildfires and high seas bring about a cataclysm it may well herald the second coming and – to the minds of many with strong faith – their own salvation. All of which presents itself as a reality in the final book of The Old Testament. Concern about climate change and faith in the second coming do not have to be identifiers of different communities, and they often weren't a few decades ago. Internet use and the advent of digital communications have greatly changed that dynamic.

One thing the internet offers us is a chance to build an identity, virtually at least. A unifier in many of the examples we have seen, from the physicist Christopher, amazed more by holding the hand of the person he loved than he was by the results in the search for dark matter, via Jennifer the Downs Syndrome girl who encountered Elvis at the moment of death and back to Roger Ascham's reverie observing the intricacies of nature in front of him, is the way each of those individuals are at once completely involved in their strange realities and also aware they are facing something bigger than themselves. Something they can't hope to fully grasp in that moment. Much of our online experience is

128

designed to reward a small amount of uncertainty in us with a readily available explanation. When we join an existing social media group because we have a shared interest, we often find the group has a long history of discussing and reenforcing its values. Such experiences help us build an identity and find others who share our experiences. Perhaps, more accurately, they give us the means to explain who we are and reward us instantly with responses to build this sense of identity. There are plenty of arguments in the world of facts and research suggesting some of what we experience online, certainly in terms of friendships and a sense of belonging might be an illusion. Anthropologist Robin Dunbar is often cited in such debates on the back of his research in the 1990s which produced "Dunbar's number." The number – 150 – is one he arrived at by considering the size and processing capacity of the human brain. Considering the way humans exist in communities, Dunbar's number is his research-based supposition of the maximum number of people with whom we could maintain a stable social relationship. It's also less than half of the average number of "friends" linked to each Facebook user in the third decade of this century. Dunbar's work is complex and considers the needs of a community and how such groups behave [5]. By contrast, most Facebook users have some connections they use sparingly with neither side being particularly motivated to get more involved. However, many people experience strong physical stresses linked to the impact they make on social media. The numbers of people prepared to interact is often understood as a measure of a person's self-worth.

Another key difference between the communities traditionally studied by anthropologists and online communities is what people mean in discussion. Very often exchanges about politics, religion or other belief systems when carried out online are really about people asserting a collective identity. The opinions expressed are more a simple set of core beliefs to hold an online community in place rather than something to be moved forward and explored. In the early sixties Canadian academic Marshall McLuhan coined the term "global village" to describe the way electronic media was uniting the world and allowing for a transfer of cultural ideas. For him, this was often a case of the United States distributing its ideology by way of exporting television programs and films. By the second decade of this century some of the more evangelical writers supporting the latest communication technology were openly considering it as way beyond sharing culture. They saw it as a power that would change and evolve us. Laurence Scott's The Four-Dimensional Human: Ways of Being in the Digital World (2016) advances the concept of "everywhereness" to describe our ability to be present wherever other humans might interact with us. To Scott, social media "encourages us to narrate our lives as legibly as possible, as ongoing books that invite themselves to be read." He also considers the way internet realities have heralded paradoxes and shifts in the way we perceive subjects. The notion of the online experience permanently packing "an acute sense of an ending and also a sense of never-ending" neatly summarises the way we constantly look for results, and sense ourselves as permanently involved in a process. The way the internet hypes up the moment and the most lurid insights is explored in Stone's discussion of the ubiquity of the "-porn" suffix when applied to subjects like the ownership of property. Many other writers have addressed the same issue with the current debates showing the sector developing its own growing language. Terms like content creator, influencer and acronyms like SEO are the best known of a raft of names either appropriated from other areas of life or developed as shorthand descriptions of the way the online world is shaping humanity. Scott uses the World's encroaching desert – i.e., a symptom of climate change - as a metaphor for the way four-dimensional existence is taking over human lives. [6]

Stone is typical of one body of academic thought, aware of the potential pitfalls of moving so much of our lives into the virtual realm, but essentially an optimist and someone for whom the opportunities of the new frontier are almost certain to shape our evolution. The potential of digital technology to take us to new realities isn't in question. It is also widely accepted that our own evolution as humans is being impacted by tech developments. A much more pressing question in terms of who we are as a species is the extent to which we are prepared and already adapted for the changes being wrought by the tech sector. In a widely quoted thought from a debate at the Harvard Museum, double Pulitzer Prize winning scientist Edward O Wilson stated: "The real problem of humanity is the following: we have Paleolithic emotions, medieval institutions, and god-like technology." Wilson's concerns go to the heart of a debate about how far we accept ourselves as four-dimensional. The titles of Wilson's later works tell their own story about his concerns; The Meaning of Human Existence (2014), Half-Earth: Our Planet's Fight for Life (2016), Genesis: The Deep Origin of Societies (2019). Born in 1929 Wilson lived long enough to see a term he coined – Biodiversity –

become a shorthand for effective management of the environment. His worries about the threat of technology overwhelming our organic foundations are rooted in an awareness that the physical and mental health of a species can easily become the casualties of carelessness.

There is no shortage of information online about the meaning of our existence or the history of our species as social animals. The issue as we process and make sense of this is really one of whether we also gain the experiences to go with the knowledge on offer, and whether without the experiences the knowledge could ever be the same. Even an optimist like Laurence Scott considers the extent to which abstaining from online activity can "trump" the claims of others to be worldly. [7] and he echoes a point made by Barry Lopez in his multi-award-winning Arctic Dreams: Imagination and Desire in a Northern Landscape (1986). Lopez spends much time pondering on the value of wilderness to the human imagination. He considers the way humans who will never visit a particular place can feel benefit from the knowledge that wilderness areas exist. His book may be within living memory but the concept of anywhere on earth existing beyond our ability to see it and respond is truly a quaint notion today. Our palaeolithic emotions remain reactive to those compelling moments when hunting is required, or danger and death present themselves. We are still required to work consciously if we want to develop bonds with our fellow humans over other things, like cultural choices. However, that is becoming easier. A generation ago someone in a small minority would struggle to find recognition and reinforcement for their beliefs. The internet has changed that. I can date one experience for me to the spring of 1981, specifically the time I walked into Track Records' shop in York, pulled a Wild Man Fischer album and Furious Pig 12" single from the racks and took my cultish uneasy listening choices to the counter. The assistant took long looks at both before entering them in the till and remarked "I told the manager we should get this stuff; I knew someone would buy it!" There was one of me in every town in those days and if we met in any meaningful sense, it involved either crowding into backstreet venues or swapping cassette tapes and notes in the post. Our beliefs were only reinforced if we made significant efforts.

*Larry "Wild Man" Fischer, uneasy listening at its best!*

Today I get away with playing the same kind of sounds in a show over the internet and people I'll never meet whose details I will never really know send me the odd message to say thank you. Collectively we're cultish but essentially harmless, and the opportunities offered to our creative heroes by the burgeoning technology of file- sharing and easily constructed online hubs is enabling to the point more fringe musicians than ever before can call themselves professionals. Where such activity is concerned four-dimensional humanity has indeed developed communities, changing lives in the process. But it has also enabled the live streaming of murderous shootings, the widespread dissemination of beheading videos and a range of other items rightly identified as capable of "radicalising." Considered as evidence of our palaeolithic brains at work my trip to acquire the vinyl few others wanted owed a lot to the hunting and gathering instinct, even if I thought it was about prizing musical artists few others regarded with any affection. I was responding to the signals of the organisation of a shop and the album cover art on display to ensure a fruitful scavenge. The extreme political violence shown online that begets more extreme political violence is appealing to a personal and provably dangerous instinct in some that also goes back to the

136

palaeolithic component of our brains, but it's a much darker element. It is of concern to lawmakers because – potentially – it influences a stage of mental development that determines the character of an individual. It may be the extreme elements of humanity that create and respond to such content but the process of desensitisation that gets us that far has many other applications. These applications drive the expansion of activity online and concern some tech insiders to the point they have driven campaigns and action. Tristan Harris is one vocal critic of the methods big tech firms use to gain and maintain attention and involvement from users. A Stanford Graduate with a stellar career that had taken him to a Product Management position at Google, Harris' life changed from the moment in 2013 when he circulated a memo for the urgent attention of ten selected colleagues. His "A Call To Minimise Distraction & Respect Users' Attention," went beyond his intended audience, reaching 5000 employees in total. Initially the response seemed highly positive with Harris offered a position as Google's in-house design ethicist and product philosopher. Harris soon came to feel he'd been moved to a marginal role where no support structure existed to suggest his learning and ideas would translate into practical policy decisions. He worried about many of the blatant and well-known features of the best-known providers in the sector, such as the way Linkedin demanded reciprocity from users and the habit of video platforms like YouTube of automatically loading further content after a user has opted for one item. For Harris, and other concerned tech insiders the major threat from big tech is the constant creeping of a business ethos capable of imposing itself on our free will. A simple example considered in a newspaper article quotes Harris: "A friend at Facebook told Harris that designers initially decided the notification icon, which alerts people to new activity such as 'friend requests' or 'likes', should be blue. It fit Facebook's style and, the thinking went, would appear 'subtle and innocuous.' 'But no one used it,' Harris says. 'Then they switched it to red and of course everyone used it.'" [8]

Harris' own journey took him through a period of soul searching towards being an advocate for an approach to tech development and use that considered our humanity as the primary focus. His writing and public appearances have given him a platform, and his website asks, "How do you ethically steer the thoughts and actions of two billion people's minds every day?" and reminds those who click on the home page that The Atlantic magazine once identified Harris as the "closest thing Silicon

Valley has to a conscience." He now acts as one of the managers and most prominent advocates in the Center for Humane Technology who used to announce on their homepage: "As long as social media companies profit from outrage, confusion, addiction, and depression, our well-being and democracy will continue to be at risk." Currently they've shifted this to a mission, stated in positive and pro-active terms "Our mission is to shift technology towards a more humane future that supports our well-being, democratic functioning, and shared information environment." [9]

Harris, and the organisation he continues to promote are not alone in their concerns and actions, but they are in a minority. Most of the major arguments are already in the public domain with debates about mental health and democracy being amongst the most heated. The responsibilities of big tech may be a concern. So too are the profits and reach of the major companies. These companies long ago mastered techniques for grabbing and holding our attention and rewarding us with constant results in response to actions we often perceive as trivial and harmless. If we continue with Edward O. Wilson's Paleolithic/medieval/god-like analysis of our current state this situation with big tech presents a truly unsettling picture. It suggests an economic system

139

built around our interactions with technology also benefits when the god-like technology on offer brings in profits on which it is obliged to pay little or no tax because the medieval institutions of humanity recognise limits to legal territories because – being largely based in national laws - they observe borders on the ground. So, companies benefit massively when they locate their management in the most amenable locations for their tax liabilities and then gather their profits from everywhere. This isn't by any means a system unique to big tech, but the toys provided by big tech mean that Laurence Scott's "everywhereness" translates, literally, into situations in which a mobile phone in a major city orders a product or service from a franchise that delivers with a contracted worker whilst the owner of the franchise manages the resulting profits in an offshore account.

It's a mysterious process but only in the sense that the deliberately opaque accounting that handles the operation and the answerability for any responsibilities it may have has been designed for maximum financial benefit and legal protection of those running the operation. We've come a long way from mystery as something with a mystic element because we've come a long way from community. In this reality the sense of connection is based on the shortest and most efficient means of monetising some human need. One practical example of this power in action occurs when stories suddenly overwhelm the news media, and the internet allows everyone with an opinion access to an audience. The disappearance of Nicola Bulley in January 2023 prompted such a frenzy. The 45-year- old mother of two vanished leaving her phone still logged in to a work call and her dog on a riverbank in Lancashire. When initial searches failed to find any trace of her the internet was soon rife with suggestions of her fate. Conspiracy theories extended to include the companies employing her and her partner, and some soon became linked to wider webs of conspiracy with their own online following. Other unofficial investigations implicated her partner. On the ground local police and members of the public in St Michaels on Wyre, where Nicola lived and disappeared, became annoyed at the number of unofficial reporters turning up to film, live-stream and gather evidence in the area. Intruding in some cases on private property and breaking into buildings. On 19 February, a little over three weeks after her disappearance, Nicola's body was found in the river, confirming what the police had always seen as the most likely scenario. Speaking through a police liaison officer and talking about the two young daughters Nicola left behind her family hit out at media intrusion, taking a particular sideswipe at the unofficial reporting, "it saddens us to think that one day we will have to explain to them that the press and members of the public accused their dad of wrongdoing, misquoted and vilified friends and family.

"This is absolutely appalling - they have to be held accountable. This cannot happen to another family." [10]

Nicola Bulley's family were unwitting fodder for an industry that thrives on its ability to offer answers and solutions. Perhaps, more accurately, the army of countless citizen journalists and theorists offer answers that make sense to their audience and confirm ideas held by audience members. The easy access to social media and website building technology that under-pins the industry has changed the way most of the developed world keeps in touch with current events and has also shifted billions of dollars towards those capable of providing the technology sustaining this situation. The case of Nicola Bulley shows the hunger for answers that drives much of this business. It also prompted a public debate. Evan Harris, who served as director of the campaign group Hacked Off (an organisation campaigning to restrict the powers of those reporting

142

on private lives and bring it regulation when they breach guidelines) said: "There's one big difference between the people on social media, who I condemn, and newspapers.

"That's the editor. These purport to be an edited, curated product, therefore they can be regulated and they should be regulated. It's hard to regulate a bloke in his basement." [11]

There's nothing new in humanity's concerns about new technologies or its abilities to misunderstand or misjudge their use. The notion of a telephone in every town seemed a positive ambition when the invention was first patented. Even further back Native Americans were initially distrustful of photography. Some of them believing each image created was a small theft of part of a soul. There have been moral panics in recent memory centred around the power of the media. In the United States rock music has battled strong Christian belief with a constant fear that the music and its culture encouraged immorality. The most famous such eruption of concern came with early rock 'n' roll but the counterculture of the sixties brought a more political angle to such worries when the cutting-edge music of the time appeared as an open invitation to take drugs and oppose America's involvement in the

Vietnam War. Even when the music was long settled down to becoming a major earner for the corporate media there were still febrile outbursts – notably the one concerning alleged backward masking (insertion of messages which could be decoded when recordings were played backwards) and other supposedly satanic elements. Jacob Aranza's book Backward Masking Unmasked (1983) documents a high-point in the hysteria as does the fall-out from the suicide pact agreed in 1985 by 18-year-old Raymond Belknap and 20-year-old James Vance from Sparks, Nevada. A drug and alcohol binge preceded their combined attempt to kill themselves with a shotgun. The fact that Vance survived with major facial disfigurements meant he was capable of sharing that the pair had listened to the music of Judas Priest prior to blasting themselves in the head. Five years later Judas Priest were in court charged that hidden messages in their music had driven the pair to their self-destructive actions. By this time complications from the damage done on the day of the suicide pact had claimed the life of Vance. The court ruled Priest had no case to answer, identifying the source of the alleged hidden messages as little more than misheard sounds and mistakes made whilst mixing backing vocals on the tracks apparently responsible for encouraging Belknap and Vance. [12]

The verdict tested the factual basis of the moral panic but, predictably, didn't stop it.

Collectively all the concerns and panics about the impact of technology, the media or any other major threat to social order can't possibly be true because some contradict each other. Many more are logically inconsistent or so badly supported, lacking even circumstantial evidence, they never gain any credibility beyond a small following. However, a few truths emerge from even this cursory glance that teach us something significant about mystery. As humans we are pre-disposed towards seeing patterns and recognising some sense in them. Five years after the Judas Priest trial psychologist Diana Deutsch devised an algorithm capable of delivering "phantom words" and phrases. Her work involved sending the same phrase of word or syllable sounds through a pair of stereo speakers with the timing offset slightly. She showed that listeners soon discerned phrases when they listened to the sounds and, also that the words and phrases they reported hearing varied. It could often be demonstrated that a particular person within the experiment heard sounds or phrases that had a specific meaning linked to something on the mind of that listener in that moment. Deutsch was delving into a phenomenon often dubbed auditory pareidolia. An offshoot of the better understood and

145

documented pareidolia – the visual perception most people recognise when they see shapes in inanimate objects like clouds.

*A potato, the way Wikipedia demonstrates Pareidolia*

[13] The current situation with mobile phones being ubiquitous across most of the world and mass access to the internet for most of the world's population is relatively new. In some ways it simply extends the mass media access most of those alive today in western countries have taken for granted throughout their lives. In other ways it puts the patterns of behaviour developed in that period in a new context. Humanity's media age represents less than one quarter of one percent of known human history. Therefore, the consideration we have already given to our past as tribal and dependent entirely on our natural environment matters because our evolutionary adaptations have almost entirely come from the more than 99% of that element of our ancestry. Manipulations from previous innovations in mass media have certainly changed our world but we have also developed enough in the way of critical faculties to be able to ignore the most lurid tabloid headlines and we survive perfectly well without reading every book that screams in large letters about its ability to change our life on its cover. The major difference between these screams for attention and our time online is the ability of the virtual tools now deployed to gain our eyeballs and ears to tap into the very patterns in our brain that evolved for other uses and convince us to continue offering up our time and

147

attention. It's a situation made all- the-more complex because national laws relating to what you can or can't publish are largely powerless against internet giants. Similarly, the blurring of boundaries regarding the purpose of online platforms means our patterns of learning and making sense have changed significantly in the present century. Facebook continues to claim itself as a social network whereby individuals can form friendships. However, when people offer up reports of events or share opinions and sources of information with like-minded followers their behaviour often morphs to resemble the work usually done by news organisations and publishers. A watershed moment in the way facts are consumed arguably occurred after the inauguration of Donald Trump as President of the United States when Kellyanne Conway, serving as Senior Counselor to the President, responded to press comments about the attendance at Trump's inauguration. Sean Spicer, Trump's press secretary had indicated the turnout was larger than Obama had enjoyed. Ariel photographs and on the ground observations suggested otherwise. Conway defended Spicer by indicating there were "alternative facts" something she later clarified as "additional facts and alternative information." Her comments saw her widely mocked in the news media and online but also marked a moment when an online community gathered in huge numbers behind the new president and staff, many of these supporters going on to mistrust the news outlets that had traditionally been the most trusted sources of information.

A concern amongst many mental health professionals is the extent to which people are now unable to defend themselves psychologically against the cascade of content that appeals to us by bypassing our rational thinking. Images including deep fake generations are so convincing as to be undetectable and much argumentative material and apparently simple facts are not what they seem. Such "facts" can be accepted when an online group all appear to be supporting them. Sites like this-person-does-not-exist.com (which is exactly what you might imagine it to be) are a window into a potential future world of fakery capable of testing our cognitive apparatus to destruction. Apps like reface are already widely used, often to create widespread amusement as users of social media sites reface themselves into famous film clips. Such clips generate many likes. They also point to the power of the widely available technology and its potential for misuse. History suggests the moral panics and dystopian visions of our past were largely overblown reactions and we wrestled most of the threats under control in the end, albeit often at a cost to ourselves and our societies.

It is notable that in the present debate many of the most evangelical advocates for the new technologies argue individual freedom and the right to choose, whilst the most vehement critics think about the needs of communities and countries. Andrew Keen's The Internet is not the Answer (2015) covered much of the concerns that now fuel campaigns to rein in the freedom of big tech and unlimited expressions of opinion online. "We all step into this brave new world" he notes; and face a "challenge". Like many of the most concerned Keen doesn't see apathy and impartiality as realistic choices when we already have a world in which more people have cell phones than have access to a flushing toilet. Keen's worry is that we have no models or precedents that give us a clear picture of where this situation ends. He worries that the present circumstance where big operations – like Google – wield massive power presents a "recursive, circular structure" that simply reinforces inequality when "data factories are eating the world" and we all become unpaid content providers for the social media networks mining our data. Keen – in common with other critics in this debate – advocates regulation and political actions as the likeliest routes to bringing the worst excesses under control. [14]

One innovative approach to engaging an audience in combating the worst excesses of fake news and online misinformation was pioneered at the University of Cambridge. The game, Go Viral developed by Dr Sander van der Linden challenges players to step into the shoes of a fake news producer and then build a career by going through the motions of spreading fake content online. The challenge is to grow an audience within the game without compromising their trust in the credibility of your content. The skills of fakery are central to success in the challenge with skills, like the creation of deepfake content, being vital to your chance to win. The aim of the game is ultimately to make players more critical of fake content. The game draws some of its design from the techniques of preventative medicine, crudely taking the same approach as an anti-viral shot, in which a weakened dose of the dangerous invader is introduced to a body to prompt the production of anti-bodies. Dr van der Linden explained the outcome to The Economist as everyone becoming their own "bullshit detector". [15] A growing group of tech talents have set out to bring ethics and honesty to their craft with many working as consultants and designers. The statement on the homepage of the Thoughtful Technology Project is typical of the broad aims found in a number of such operations: "Our information ecosystem determines who we trust, who we hate, who we vote for, the decisions we make, and even what wars we fight.

"The Thoughtful Technology Project aims to ensure that emerging technology does not irreversibly harm our information ecosystem — that we use our new powers wisely to build a positive future." [16] Research on the Go Viral game suggests it is most effective when used like a vaccine, including being offered as a regular booster after the initial application. The World Health Organisation are counted amongst its supporters.

Many are alarmed by the notion of irreversible harm of both our information ecosystem, and our critical faculties as humans. The worry is not limited to the tech sector. The innovations and good intentions of the ethical tech entrepreneurs will not succeed on their own. The biggest blows that might be dealt to the massive powers of the tech giants – the forced breaking up of monopolies and imposition of harsher business and tax regulations – are frequently discussed. Any regulatory moves are likely to be powerfully resisted within big tech.

Mystery, and the experience of mystery are notable casualties in much of the experience offered online.

152

For as long as the situation outlined in this chapter continues mystery remains under threat as a human experience in the 21$^{st}$ century. Perhaps more accurately mystery is a casualty of the way we are now encouraged to interact. The most effective and addictive online behaviours are those that generate a small amount of physical response and prompt some immediate action. The predominance of cute cat videos on our social media, for example. Those initial responses can trigger the palaeolithic portion of ourselves to perceive itself as involved in a process, at which point we tend to follow further triggers to more content. We may investigate the mysterious in such circumstances but the extent to which we experience some sense of being involved in a deep mystery is questionable.

The processes involved greatly resemble the way the mysterious has always been part of our cultural experience. Some personal experiences of mine suggest the differences between the past and present in the way we involve ourselves in mystery and the way we now understand it. Firstly, I have spoken at paranormal events and to groups of people for a decades, my main subject being UFOs. The advent of the internet hit the market for such work. A commercial high-point of the mid 1990s, coincided with popularity of the X-Files television series and
153

the sudden drop in costs of magazine production. This meant that articles, live talks, and books were all profitable. A few years later much content was online, and the most popular material was, predictably, that suggesting widespread conspiracies and massive coverups. I moved on to writing on other subjects though I never stopped involving myself by way of keeping up to date with serious research on the subject. Returning to conferences and talks late in the second decade of this century I was struck by how much of the "merch" sections of the events were offering self-published material produced with the aid of the online facilities offered by the likes of Lulu.com and Amazon. A predictable moan from those of us with a background in academia being that this growing trend was increasing the amount of poorly evidenced and poorly expressed argument in the market. The "market" in this case being a niche area, subject to periodic explosions of sales when a phenomenon, like the popularity of the X-Files, boosts interest. This observation is relevant to a debate on mystery because a significant portion of the audience for content on the best-known mysteries are looking for answers. A segment of those searching for answers are people who have had their own uncanny and highly mysterious experience. As we have seen, the

154

mental effort of believing falls far short of the effort required to continue questioning and remain sceptical. A lot of self-published material exists because the authors in question have their own clear answer and couldn't find a commercial publisher willing to get behind their work. The unwillingness of the commercial publishers in such cases is prompted by their own reaction to manuscripts which appear to lack rigour. This may be an uncharitable review of a robust little section of the market for self-published works but the point I'm making is that the silo effect seen when like-minded people congregate online also applies to physical media and one casualty of this is the debate within communities about complex subjects. The definitive proof on many of the world's longest established mysteries and mystic experiences continues to elude us. One reason for that is that we are currently more likely than at any time to find answers that feel right momentarily and trust our own momentary reaction. We're very used to this instinctive feeling because it's the same rapid progression from hunch to certainty we feel when researching other questions online, like trying to find a good cat hotel or buy an effective brand of weed killer.

The process mimics a social phenomenon that has been known and celebrated throughout living memory, but crucially differs in one key element of this. It lacks the nuanced detail that reminds the audience member that they, too, have power to make sense of what they're being told. I grew up in Cumbria and every year the local media celebrated the annual World's Biggest Liar competition held in the Bridge Inn, Santon Bridge. The village has one pub and a population a little over 300 so in many ways still resembles the picture it presented in the 19th century when the legendary Will Ritson was landlord of the pub. The competition is held in fond memory of Ritson whose famous lies included the claim the Lake District turnips grew so big some had been carved out to form cow sheds. The competition has moved with the times in some ways, offering up its first foreign winner in 2003 and first female winner – comedian Sue Perkins - in 2006.

*Sue Perkins, champion liar 2006*

However, the sense of celebrating the essence of a good story and the subversive celebration of truthfulness within a tall tale has always been a central element of the celebration of storytelling. One legend, believed but unproven, suggests: "It is told that the Bishop of Carlisle happened to be passing one year and went up to the crowd to lecture them on the evils of lying. He ended his speech with 'for my part I have never told a lie in my life,' and was unanimously awarded first prize which was thrown into his carriage." [17]

The scurrilous celebration of truthfulness within complex lies was part of my growing up in the county and often expressed when adults told children unbelievable tales, the point of which was partly entertainment and partly to boost critical thinking. Years later, reading a biography of film star James Dean I found a discussion of a similar competition that took place where he grew up in Fairmount, Indiana. One common feature of that competition and the one in Cumbria was the prevalence of local historians amongst the entrants and winners. In other words, those most trusted and respected to handle factual details were also conspicuously successful liars. Indeed, they were respected as such. This isn't as surprising as it might seem. Storytelling traditions exist where an understanding of truth and

158

reality is multi-layered, extending beyond facts to include moral components and often insights into the less savoury aspects of personal behaviour. The 2011 World's Biggest Liar – Glen Boylan – won with a story about betting on a snail race with Prince Charles, the then heir to the throne apparently advising him to remove the shell to make his snail more aerodynamic, only for Boylan to lose when his opponents cheated with battery-operated snails. Superficially it's surreal nonsense. But, in an era that saw the disgrace of drug-assisted sporting champions like Lance Armstrong and a conspiracy theory arguing Michael Schumacher's first F1 world championship was achieved partly by technical cheating Boylan's snail story also resonates. It speaks to deeply human concerns about our willingness to sink to moral transgressions and ruthlessness when a massive prize might be the result.

Such stories form a substantial element of what we understand as mystery. I researched a group of these tales in compiling a book about the myths and legends attaching themselves to The Beatles. One of the best known of these myths being the glorious wrong-headed wonder suggesting Paul McCartney died in November 1966 and was replaced by William Campbell "Billy" Shears, who has passed himself off successfully ever since. Improbably, in 1969 the tale enjoyed such high profile it was debated on prime-time American television and Life magazine despatched a photographer to locate McCartney, then holed up on his remote farm on Scotland's Mull of Kintyre. It's extremely entertaining nonsense which – should you be that way inclined – may lead you to hours of fun applying a mirror to the drum on the front cover of the Sgt Pepper album, listening intently to some of the most unlistenable snatches of late-period Beatle output and paying close attention to Paul's top lip in photographs taken before and after November 1966. A few lesser-known elements of this tale include the fact that Beatles' press officer, Derek Taylor took a very relaxed view of the whole affair and that the band's older albums began climbing the US charts in the wake of the rumour. Considered in the context of the World's Biggest Liar it's easy to see a pattern in the Paul is dead rumour that underlies this "evidence." Much of the hysteria was celebrated for the amusing but improbable baloney it always was. But it came from an era when rock albums were treasured possessions, much more expensive in real terms than they are today. 1969 was somewhere around the high-water mark for a period in which albums might appear as brilliant missives from visionary talents. Marijuana had been available and celebrated for many years but its widespread availability and its role as something akin to a sacrament amongst the counter cultural generation was a new development, and of great concern to middle America in particular. The late sixties reality of stoned hippie coteries imbibing smoke and sounds as their free ranging minds contemplated the meaning of life gives some context to the fleeting dead Beatle legend. From a business point of view, it's also worth remembering that the only reliable means most of them had of investigating the alleged hidden messages was to physically manipulate vinyl albums on their own turntables. There is no statistic chronicling how many of the old Beatle albums re-scaling the charts in 1969 were purchased as replacements for copies destroyed in impulsive attempts to prove the Paul rumour one way or the other. It is, however, true that sales figures for the period were a pleasant surprise for Capitol in the USA and Parlophone in Britain. [16] It's also impossible to record at this distance to what extent the messages "heard" by those taking an interest in the subject were the result of confirmation bias regarding something they really wanted to hear or audio pareidolia, again attaching itself to some concern on their mind. Ironically one person who reported such an effect was McCartney himself, discussing the hysteria a few years after it had died down. One belief amongst some avid listeners to Sgt Pepper concerned an alleged pornographic message disguised in the final seconds of the album: "Some fans came around to my door giggling. I said, 'Hello, what do you want?' They said, 'Is it true, that bit at the end? Is it true? It says 'We'll fuck you like Supermen.' I said, 'No, you're kidding. I haven't heard it, but I'll play it.' It was just some piece of conversation that was recorded and turned backwards. But I went inside after I'd seen them and played it seriously, turned it backwards with my thumb against the motor, turned the motor off and did it backwards. And there it was, sure as anything, plain as anything. 'We'll fuck you like Supermen.' I thought, Jesus, what can you do?" [19]

The Paul is dead rumour is useful as an insight into the workings of mystery because as a here and gone hysteria it's a microcosmic study of some of the workings of the way a good legend is passed around. These days the focus is on the facts that fuelled the story, The Beatles' decision to stop touring in late 1966 being key to the way myths about their lives built up. Around 1969 much of the fuss was down to the sheer fun of older initiates calmly involving younger, and altogether more gullible types into the mystery by way of cosy sessions in bedrooms with record players listening intently to Beatle recordings.

162

The involvement of stimulants, legal and otherwise, also played a part. As with the World's Biggest Liar competition, this legend survived because of underlying truths. The underlying truths have nothing to do with the actual death of Paul McCartney but do teach us a lot about the way the most dedicated fans are capable of conceiving of their idols as people with phenomenal powers.

Mysteries and lies are not the same thing but they do overlap where legend or humour addresses a deep truth. Comedian Billy Connolly tackled this in one of his most celebrated performances: "I should tell you I lie a lot...I have made myself very windswept and interesting, as the years have gone on. Because I was born a sort of fart. So, I've tried everything to be exotic. I've fought being plain all my life, but it keeps coming back. I always look... when I buy something expensive, I look as if I stole it.

"That's another thing I love...it's adverts. I love the lie. I like lies on that scale, especially... cause there's nothing wrong with lies, they're fabulous things. My God, I'm a liar for a living!" [20]

Humour remains one of our greatest mysteries, largely because the theories produced to explain it often feel partially satisfying. Crudely, we laugh when things are incongruous or surprising and when the

163

jokes allow us to feel superior. It's no accident that things that terrify us, like sex and death, are perennial subjects of humour. But – fundamentally – humour, like most of our great art, speaks to something honest and human, even when it comes at it from an unexpected angle. Billy Connolly's "I'm a liar for a living!" celebration of his art places himself in the context of the embellished claims made by advertisers, it rewards his audience for their critical ability to understand what lies beneath both adverts and his comedy. There has always been concern about advertising and humour. In the case of adverts the concerns about honesty and accuracy never go away. Similarly, the issue of what "jokes" are acceptable is always up for discussion. These areas touch on our understanding of mystery because there is a permanent dynamic in which we are always smaller than those selling us things or trying to make us laugh, but also powerful in that we make choices and give value to their attempts. At the same time, the adverts and jokes surprise us with ideas capable of testing the limits of our thinking. We have critical faculties that give us control. We also realize there are others out there with the same critical faculties making other choices. We might not agree with them, but we exist side-by-side. For example, however much some people find so-called sick humour distasteful the internet has seen an explosion of opportunities to share such jokes and on 25 June 2009, when Michael Jackson died one enduring repository of tastelessness – the Sickipedia – crashed because so many people were motivated to post jokes at his expense.

It may have been far from perfect, but the post-war western world exhibited enough tolerance and unity to survive massive social changes and produce more political stability, particularly regarding the absence of wars, than the previous century had seen. A significant part of the political understanding under-pinning this was exhibited in the effort to establish international political consensus through bodies like the United Nations. The disagreements and ongoing fractious debates recorded in the archives of the UN don't do justice to a simple point about these multi-national organisations. At heart the likes of the UN and World Health Organisation (WHO) are expressions of a basic humanity. They don't realistically expect to agree politically and most of the seasoned campaigners functioning within them expect regular political interference and disappointment. But they exist partly because all of those involved accept that nurturing our humanity is a bigger cause than any political agenda. Crudely, recognising our shared history and uniting to ensure

165

all that we have gained contributes to improving our experience as a species in the future. A recognition and celebration of mystery is not written into the constitution of any of these multi-national agencies. However, it is there, in spirit at least, because accepting that political goals and personal agendas are smaller and less significant than this shared humanity is also a celebration of the mysterious. Apart from anything else, being respectful of a shared humanity when we struggle to define exactly what it is that we share means the lofty goals of an organisation like the United Nation take on the same kind of moral codes that under-pin the major religions of the world. That point – at least – is proven by the fact that much of the most vehement criticism directed at such bodies is unleashed when individual agendas are seen to pollute the common good.

Fundamental to mystery and the experience of mystery is the recognition in the moment of encountering the mysterious that we are facing something larger than ourselves and impossible to understand in a simple way. William James' codification of the mystic experience lined up four defining aspects. To James, mystic experience is ineffable (i.e., more about feeling than intellect), "noetic" (i.e., capable of imparting knowledge),

166

transient (there and gone rapidly) and passive (because it typically finds us when we aren't seeking it). However much we try to manage our life experiences in terms of surrounding ourselves with the right friends, favourite music, best locations and readily available food and drink, it is still the case that the best moments in our memories tend to emerge in a way that fits the model of mysticism. Jokes, in fact, are a good example of such because they rely so much on context. Billy Connolly's words above are funnier delivered by the garishly dressed comedian sporting, as he did in 1986, a haircut more fashionable ten years earlier. The "liar for a living!" line works because he embodies the statement. Placed on a comedy bill with the cream of the talent culled from years of the Oxford and Cambridge Footlights (i.e., members of the Monty Python team and people like Alan Bennett), Connolly once joked he was the only person on stage that night who had "left school before I was 21." Comedy is arguably the most subjective of all arts but when Channel Four polled people to identify the best stand-up comedian in 2007 Connolly topped the list of 100 performers. In the case of both performances cited here Connolly's audience bought into a widely known history in which the comedian had worked his way from a shipyard welder to earn the right to front "An

Audience With…" the USP of which was the chance of seeing a celebrity being admired by fellow professionals.

When Edward O. Wilson identified our palaeolithic brains, he was referring to the developments that got humanity from the period 3.3 million years ago to around 10,000 years ago. A period marked by the advancement of tools and technology, organised foraging and significant developments in culture including symbolic communication and social cohesion. History frequently presents past epochs in the context of them lacking the things that define the present. It is easy to miss the fact that our palaeolithic brains – which evolved as different human variants competed for supremacy – are the result of successful adaptations. They helped us survive then, and their usefulness is not extinguished today. These are the brains that built our religions and identity. They are not, necessarily, the brains that big tech companies or a few others competing for our eyeballs and ears want us to use all day, every day.

The nameless aide to George W Bush who derided the "reality-based community" did so at the start of an era when powerful algorithms began directing us to online content capable of stimulating users to continue clicking and consuming. There have been worries that other media content over the years was addictive and harmful, but "clickbait" is amongst the most successful. Once it became an accepted and distinct reality, we felt the need of a new and appropriately compact word to describe it. We needed the word just like we needed to redefine the meaning of "lockdown" in the face of the Covid-19 pandemic because the new reality was sufficiently different to what had gone before to require new terminology and new nuances in our understanding. The practices that prompted the likes Tristan Harris to inject more ethicality into the attention economy are often those that give us some semblance of mystery in its widest form. Algorithms are at their most effective when we feel a physical urge and find ourselves eager to access the content beckoning one click away. In those moments we can easily watch the spectacular accident without experiencing the motor race in the company of others or enjoy another few seconds of a clever cat flushing a toilet. As we do this our data is downloaded by others. Our palaeolithic brains react to the danger in the accident, or feeling of love for the cat and recognise also we are in the presence of a bigger reality, like death or the need to nurture. But, often, online that's all they do. We are more effective consumers in the attention economy when we're not encouraged to articulate or explore those recognitions beyond another click and another feeding of the need for novelty. We're good customers in this reality because we often don't perceive ourselves as customers.

Mystery – in its widest definition – is under threat for the obvious reasons when you compare our current realities to the examples from the past we have already seen. There are no more hours in a day than there ever were and the tonnage of time devoted to mobile phone use or the range of other screens that fill our working and leisure time often pitches us into the repetitive and diverting behaviours that feed us facts, or what we perceive to be facts, and a diet of experience richer in novelty and distraction than any epoch has ever encountered. Our brain chemistry and the functions of the different areas of our brains have both evolved to the point our species exists and survives with the new reality. Perhaps more accurately, we are still here and inhabiting the world. We can often feel like we are coping but we recognise that much of that ability to cope is a compromise between surviving in our current world by meeting demands whilst at the same time feeling like we are growing as individuals. The 10,000 years since the end of the palaeolithic age is a little more than a moment in evolutionary history and our adaptations to new realities haven't moved quickly enough to cope with new technologies or new aspects to the organisation of the working world. In countries like the UK the casualty count of those who don't feel as if they are coping is told partly in the statistics of mental health referrals. I once investigated the situation – regarded as a crisis by some I interviewed – for a local paper. The situation in the town I researched in 2018 largely matched the reports appearing in the national media at the time. The one significant difference I found was that my local area, thankfully, wasn't keeping pace with the national rise in suicides amongst the under 40s. However, one local funeral director took time to explain to me that her business had seen a significant increase of people dying because they chose lifestyles with little heed of the dangers. Simply, these deaths were people who had felt their stake in society was so marginal they'd drunk or drugged themselves into health problems that considerably shortened their lives. Elsewhere in researching the article, massive rises in anxiety, and more complex mental health conditions were often the result of people striving very hard to achieve targets or feel like they had some foothold on a social ladder but falling foul of a working world that offered zero hours contracts and few opportunities to build a genuine career. With education beyond the age of 18 coming with a massive price tag and tough competition for the few opportunities that presented a clear escape route from the situation, a great many of those referring themselves, or exhibiting the levels of self-harm or mental distress that got them referred by others, felt trapped. The levels of anxiety resulting from these situations are known to generate the stress hormone cortisol and drive the "fight or flight" responses in our brains that evolved to help our ancestors cope with the dangers of an environment way beyond their control.

There's a certain irony in the thought of someone comfortably housed, regularly employed and in no danger of starvation suffering such anxieties that they can't sleep, and then plunging into circular thinking whereby worrying about not sleeping is a major cause of being unable to sleep. I heard such stories researching the article and wasn't surprised when I did. Our fight or flight response is clearly still very effective when people find it working overtime in such situations despite the absence of any close physical danger.

One similarity between the people on the receiving end of the mental health problems I investigated and those thriving on the awe walks described by Virginia Sturm and Dacher Kelter is the sense for both groups of being confronted by a reality they feel is larger than themselves. The difference – in the simplest terms – between the two groups is the extent to which they feel connected to that reality. If the working world feels like a hostile environment colluding to exclude you, your own engagement with it is limited. On the small study I did the sense of being excluded or unable to achieve was a major reason for young people, particularly, to feel massively anxious. The same youngsters were also those who had grown up never knowing a world before online existence. They often lived that curious double life of appearing in a positive light on social media whilst privately admitting to FOMA (or fear of missing out) where they felt they were the only ones faking their social media positivity. This echoed something I'd seen in my life as an academic where the second decade of this century brought with it a notable rise in the number of students arriving with medical evidence relating to their mental health. The severity of the cases we dealt with was also increasing to the point that I recall an office conversation in which my little team wondered when, exactly, we'd signed up to be social workers.

The issues here are not simple. We are rich in assets and distractions, but often poor in available time. The reasons mystery is under threat are complex and the solutions (assuming we as a species are motivated to identify the threat to mystery as a problem) only work if many people involve themselves. Some solutions appear easy. But you don't provide a cure to the problems explored above by simply dragging people out into forests or dispensing with mobile phones, though you may well help individuals when you do that. As I said at the beginning of this book, this is "the literary equivalent of a talk to a group. I want to share some knowledge and insights and leave you with the information and the ideas you will require to explore the subject in more depth." Hopefully that has been achieved. I've presumed myself competent to write this short study, and stepped aside to let in someone else when I knew that would present something I couldn't explain. Nothing more. However hopeful, or pessimistic, we are about the future the truth is none of us know for certain what is coming. In that, at least, we are united in sharing an experience of being confronted by something bigger than us. Something hard to control or fully understand. In short, one of the biggest mysteries we face is understanding what our future holds.

# CHAPTER FIVE

# SO WHAT?

"Medicine and Wisdom of Old Stories for New Uncertain Times"

From homepage of Nana Tomova's website.

Usually at the end of a talk to a group there's a certain amount of discussion in which those with a particular insight or fact to share ask question, say what's on their mind or simply invite discussion. First and foremost, in the context of this book, I'd invite you to stop, think and consider the value to yourself of connecting with something mysterious. That's mysterious in the widest possible sense of the term. Anything that presents you with a reality so large and challenging that merely attempting to contain it within your sensory abilities is a challenge. That – crudely – is the under-pinning idea behind a range of initiatives that seek to protect the natural world or involve people in physical activity and encountering the outdoors. One project in the UK, based at the University of Reading sums up the health benefits of physical activity: "Not moving leads to damage from free radicals released by mitochondria in human cells. This causes premature aging and diseases such as cancer, heart disease, diabetes, dementia, and depression. There is no medication or diet that will prevent this damage. There is a simple cure though – being more active!" Intelligent Health seek to build active communities and their work is enacted in ways that link physical activity with social activity and connecting with nature. [1] They are not open advocates for promoting mystery in the way it has been discussed in the preceding trio of chapters but a useful place to start because they present a simple example of a complex phenomenon in the present day. Many projects that seek to connect people in a holistic way begin with some focus on provable outcomes, like the health benefits of exercise, but design themselves in ways allowing other, harder to define, benefits to emerge. Dr William Bird, who is central to the Intelligent Health project once discussed in a television interview the stimulation

176

afforded to the amygdala and hippocampus from activities carried out in woodlands and further highlighted the positive impact on the ability of human brains to produce alpha waves - the brain waves increased by meditation practice and associated with wakeful relaxation - that would result.

Mystery is no one thing, and the routes onward from considering mystery in isolation depend entirely on individual needs and choices. All I can usefully do as we wind down is share the kind of anecdotes and ideas that would form a typical checking out from a talk to a group. If we stick with the natural world for a moment one thing that strikes me is the way each generation has found its own way of rediscovering and re-framing our relationship with nature. The sensory input from contact with weather, plants and animals has always impacted on us. Some of this redefining has been necessary because of the open assault humans have inflicted on the natural world throughout our recorded history. The evidence of the impact is strong enough now to make clear how much it endangers the future of things we all rely on including weather patterns, the growth of crops and the stability of areas of land on which we rely, like the locations of coastal cities. To some societies of the past the gods expressed themselves in nature.
177

Items we currently take to be inanimate, like rocks, had a role in an environment that was sentient and included ourselves. These days many of the more recent expressions of our relationship with nature, especially in western countries, are by way of experiences we might regard as commodified. An example of this is the Walk in the Wild experience offered by storyteller and poet Nana Tomova in West Sussex which combines two and a half miles of wandering in Sussex's South Downs with the chance to hear stories and poetry and create your own work. There are those who would take issue with a landscape as carefully managed as the South Downs of England as a "wild" area but that's a churlish criticism in the face of an experience designed to be open ended and enlightening. In the end it's possible to gain some of the benefits of contact with nature in locations notably less wild than an English national park.

It's no accident that the commodification of our links with nature has worked its way into our media and achieved massive success in every generation. A motto of sorts referencing this constant need is outlined in Gavin Maxwell's preface for his multi-million selling Ring of Bright Water: "I am convinced that man has suffered in his separation from the soil and from other living creatures of that world; the

178

evolution of his intellect has outrun his needs as an animal, and as yet he must still, for security, look long at some portion of the earth as it was before he tampered with it." [2] Recent examples including the Blue Planet television series, or books like Helen Macdonald's H is for Hawk have often included moments when our guides have simply invited us to look and marvel along with them. In the parlance of literary criticism, we are in territory sometimes identified with the term "the figurative possibilities of failure." In simple terms this is the acceptance of the fact that no attempt to interpret can be more meaningful than simply drawing the attention of the reader or viewer to the overwhelming reality in front of you. The original experience in such cases is understood to be – partially at least - beyond words. Other successful explorations of nature include the ever popular "topographical narratives" within which people set off to explore, usually bringing some purpose of their own to the journey. In such tales the tension for the reader or viewer comes partly from an element of the unknown and some sense of investment in the narrator. The tales change with time and sometimes develop a meaning because they capture a moment. William Cobbett's rural rides took place just over two centuries ago, allowing the author to catch a snapshot of the English countryside at the time it was being depopulated as more and more people moved to a manufacturing economy based in cities and towns. Cobbett's vivid descriptions and personal affinity with the people he meets add a poignancy to this change. Raynor Winn's works The Salt Path (2018), Wild Silence (2020) and Landlines (2022), by contrast, deal with current concerns and recount long-distance walks undertaken – initially - in the light of her and her husband becoming homeless after an unsound investment. The books also chronicle their ongoing battle to cope with and contain for as long as possible his terminal illness. Amongst travellers of all levels of adventurousness and creative ability the travel blog, with its focus on scenes and key moments and its suggestion of telling a story, has become a default means of sharing. So, learning from these resources and building the lessons into our own lives is a possibility. Changing scenery, being open to nature and breathing in clean air whilst the weather expresses itself are a basic in terms of being open to a wider experience that challenges us to feel something in the moment.

We saw in chapter two that grappling with difficult questions and research is a journey into the mysterious for some. As someone who spent decades in academia, I worked in a period in which the focus on results became ever more important, both as a means by which institutions were paid and as a means by which students gauged their own views of success. The notion of studying and investigating something as a means of achieving personal growth was squeezed out of the process as a result. However, it's undervalued as a means of bringing mystery and meaning into your own personal life. The biggest mystery being you can't know where the most challenging subjects will lead you but their ability to challenge and change lives suggests they will take you somewhere. If we imagine this check out section of the book as a parting conversation then I'd share at this point that two activities of mine have been massive sources of fulfilment, learning and moments that William James could easily match against his codification of the mystic. Both are things some my own teachers suggested would be unlikely to prove profitable, either personally or financially. I gravitated towards music (rock music to start with) and wondering about UFOs because each seemed fascinating to my young self. In truth, I can't recall a time before I loved either of these things. What I see years later is that each has given me a deeper learning experience than much of what I learned in achieving qualifications. As a child I had ufology figured out in a very short time, it was clearly real aliens arriving

181

from outer space. In my defence I was somewhere around seven years old when I worked this out. Since when the subject has taught me so much about people that sometimes the alleged aliens seem irrelevant. Similarly, the most unexpected moments at live gigs have guided my life. The few acts to whom I've remained doggedly loyal are those who tend to avoid greatest hits shows or even playing the same tracks in the same order every night. DJ John Peel once remarked that all he really wanted to hear was something he hadn't heard before. Against all logic I still have that sense that the best thing I could hear might be the next thing I stumble upon. Peel didn't live to see Bandcamp where the world and his performing dog can load up all manner of audio and tag it as they see fit. The music arrives so quickly no single human could keep track of the ever-expanding catalogue or – indeed – check out whether those appearing to load black metal sounds from Tehran really do reside there and, consequently, put their liberty and physical well-being on the line by daring to record such music. Somewhere in an office the programmers of Smooth FM might look at my date of birth and income and assume I'm one of theirs. Erm, no! I'll choose mystery and surprise and share it with my handful of Smooth rejecting listeners for as long as there is still one of us in every town. Not only that but I'll find myself moved by things that effortlessly present the mysterious in an accessible way, one such being the graffiti works of CatNeil, a Margate artist who specialises in images of cats with blissful expressions and simple messages suggesting something cosmic like "The Universe is Alive". In fact, I'd even go so far to suggest that one simple avenue available to anyone in beginning to appreciate mystery is to take time to appreciate just how much readily available creative work is out there to enjoy, and in doing so make it your business to engage with the stuff that isn't expecting to find you as the audience. In the context of a brief concluding chapter to a book on mystery this matters because I'm suggesting this as a short route away from any silo of predictable opinions. Putting yourself deliberately in a situation in which there are ideas to engage you, but you're placed in a position of insignificance in terms of your understanding is inviting awe into your life. CatNeil's work did that to me simply because the first time I encountered it I realised I'd spent years trying to argue the ins and outs of big ideas relating to The Ultimate Question and it hadn't occurred to me once that graffiti on an epic scale, with a sense of humour, was an ideal means of communication.

*CatNeil, tells it like it is!*

It goes with the territory if you talk or write about the paranormal that you'll be asked about your own experiences. I'd write off the one time I was apparently communicating with aliens as an occasion in which I communicated with nothing other than a human intelligence, or two. Similarly, my best UFO sighting fits all the usual signifiers of a man-made object seen under the kind of conditions that might confuse a witness. So, I often share one moment that dragged me into the full William James checklist (uncanny, imparting knowledge, unasked for and transient) and point out that anyone bothered enough can find what I was looking at on YouTube. As paranormal experiences come this one is rooted firmly in the real world and instructive in terms of what a mysterious moment might teach. Apologies, but we're back to football again. Because, when Carlisle United, on their way to the Third Division title in the 94-95 season, faced Barnet at Brunton Park, Carlisle in the 13th game of the campaign it was a match of some significance to the division. Both teams sat in the top four that afternoon with Carlisle tottering but just hanging onto their lead. The 4-0 thumping they gave the Londoners had significance to the promotion campaign, but the second goal of the game gave me a briefly shocking experience. Paul Conway's spectacular achievement is there online this day [3] but what isn't recorded is that as soon as he got the ball, I simply felt he was going to score. Not an obvious feeling for a Carlisle fan at a game even when a begging chance occurs on the pitch but, in this instance, nothing was begging. Conway got the ball in the middle of the pitch and ran toward the Barnet goal under challenge before unleashing a perfectly timed shot that put the Cumbrians 2-0 up. There was clear potential between the centre circle and the back of the net for something to go wrong and I'm not prone to anything approaching a premonition, particularly at lower league football matches. So, all told, that uncanny feeling and the outcome of the event stayed with me as well as the satisfaction of knowing we'd sent a message to the rest of the division that afternoon. My rational explanation is that a few unusual things were combining to create that situation. Firstly, in my lifelong support of the club that season marks the strongest campaign. I went to matches knowing we had the best squad in the division with the ability to outclass opponents, a rarity in our history. A goal like that was simply more possible in that campaign. Secondly, I watched it from an unusual position in a stand along the side but towards one end of the pitch and I'd gone with people – my eldest son and my father – who didn't usually attend the games. More than anything I wanted *them* to share that experience. So, it didn't feel like my typical experience, down closer to the pitch and watching with some of the usual crowd. I don't think I saw a few seconds into the future. I do think I came to appreciate how much a few marginal bits of my consciousness combined in that moment and how much everything I sensed about the peripheral parts of a game allowed me to anticipate the outcome of something. Not so much a sixth sense as an acceptance that there are always perceptions going on that we disregard. Opening up to your marginal perceptions is the basis of a number of widely used means of getting in touch with your senses. The simplest forms of meditation encourage it and activities like forest bathing require slow breathing and the sensing of smells and sounds.

*Paul Conway scores that goal - photo courtesy of Evening News and Star, Carlisle*

Alternatively, I just got lucky, from the moment Conway got the ball there was a chance he'd be tackled or miss, but he powered through to score. Getting lucky and reading meaning into it is a very typical piece of human behaviour, notably regarding premonitions where we tend to recall when we or others got it right. A spectacular example of such success appeared to occur in September 2022 when, following the death of Queen Elizabeth II Mario Reading's book Nostradamus: The Complete Prophecies For The Future (2006) climbed the best-seller lists after it appeared to pin-point an accurate date of the monarch's death. Mario Reading himself wasn't a significant beneficiary of the luck, having died in 2017, but his book spawned yet another revival of interest in the 16<sup>th</sup> century French seer. The popularity of Nostradamus' enigmatic predictions have frequently been supported by such discoveries in which a previously hard to fathom description appears to fit a specific event. Sceptics claim the benefit of 20/20 hindsight and confirmation bias both contribute to such claims. For the purposes of the present study what matters is the ongoing fascination with all things mysterious, an area in which Nostradamus has been a proven success for centuries.

Of course, if you want to engage with mystery you can start at the other – cynical and pragmatic - end of the scale. The observation "in this world nothing can be said to be certain, except death and taxes" is typically credited to Benjamin Franklin and comes from a letter written in 1789. [4] It's a profound thought contained in pithy prose, so it's not surprising it has been repeated. Most people at some point in their lives do choose to confront the death aspect of this observation and at least think their way through what, exactly, it means to them. However far off you consider your likely death to be, there's nothing stopping you simply wading into reading, discussing, praying, experiencing in the moment, and otherwise attempting to fill your life with attempts to interrogate The Ultimate Question. Mysteries come no bigger because this one encapsulates everything discussed in this book. The best mysteries in real life are those that continually reveal how little you know, even as you wade through more and more learning and immerse yourself in more experience. That reality, ultimately, is central to the human experience. Whatever the truth about Dunbar's number, claims of paranormal experience and the health benefits to be gained from activities like awe walks it remains part of our experience that we are surrounded by more sensory experience than we can accommodate, and more mystifying knowledge than we can ever hope to retain. It is provably part of the human condition. We see an acknowledgement of our fascination with the Ultimate Question from our first recorded artefacts to the present day. This teaches us we have always been overwhelmed by aspects of our surroundings and throughout human history we have been seeking to understand who we are and what we can achieve.

This short discussion does not end with any instruction about what is right for you, individually. The point here is to argue why mystery matters. It matters that we understand what it might be, it matters much more that we embrace the mysterious and challenge ourselves in whatever ways we see fit to engage with mystery. Mystery is there in the things we don't understand, the experiences that ambush us, the things we feel strongly that we need to know, and in those truths that remain elliptical as we constantly strive to define them. It is there for all of us, it always has been and however much we work to resolve troubling questions, mystery in all its forms will be there all around us for as long as we exist. How long that will be is also a mystery.

# The Biggest Mysteries

1 - Reza Aslan – God: A Human History of Religion, Corgi 2018, p. 35

2 – Aslan, p. 59

3 – Dee Brown – Bury my Heart at Wounded Knee, Vintage 1991, pp. 431-445

4 – Robert Macfarlane – Underland, Penguin 2019, pp. 55-69

5 – William James – The Varieties of Religious Experience, Penguin Classics 1985, pp. 379-382

6 – Kevin Nelson – The God Impulse: Is Religion Hardwired into our Brains, Simon and Schuster 2011, p. 58

7 – Raymond A. Moody: Elvis After Life, Peachtree 1987, pp. 54-55

8 – Kevin Nelson, p. 104

9 – Neil Nixon, UFOs, Aliens and the Battle for the Truth, Oldcastle Books 2020, p. 29

10 - Jaques Vallee, Passport to Magonia, Neville Spearman 1970, pp. 23-25

11 – Brian Innes, Ghost Sightings: Accounts of Worldwide Paranormal Activity, Amber Books 2016, pp. 129-132

12 – John Donne, The Major Works, Oxford University Press 2008, p. 336

13 – Gerald Bullett, The English Mystics, Michael Joseph 1950, p. 99

14 – Walter J C Murray, Copsford, Little Toller Books 2019, p. 75

15 – Tom Wareham, The Green Man of Horam: The Life and Work of Walter J C Murray, self- published 2017, pp. 112-114

16 – Bertrand Russell, Mysticism and Logic, Unwin 1963, pp. 10-13

17 – Barry Lopez, Horizon, Bodley Head 2019, quotes taken from pp 28, 48 and 159

18 – The quote in this chapter comes directly from a sound clip on Gregg's website. The clip appears on a page packed with reviews of his book and discussions of the major points it contains: https://www.justingregg.com/narwhal

19 – John Gray, Straw Dogs, Granta 2002, p. 61

# Harnessing the Power of Mystery

1 – Mike Martin, The Mysterious Case of the Vanishing Genius, Psychology Today 1 May 2012

2 – Adrian Lee, Dreaming of Blighty: Newly uncovered journal reveals British PoW's fantasies, Daily Express 23 Oct 2013

3 – Tunes for Tyrants, BBC Four 2017, Episode 3

4 – Michael Williams, Superstition and Folklore, Bossiney Books 1982, p. 32

5 – Misia Landau, Narratives of Human Evolution, Yale University Press 1993

6 – Skeptoid, Podcast #721, Debunking Ancient Aliens, Part 3, March 31 2020

7 – Skeptoid, Podcast #751, Pop Quiz: Myths of the Middle Ages, Oct 27 2020

8 – Vic Tandy and Tony R. Lawrence, The Ghost in the Machine, Journal of the Society for Psychical Research, Vol.62, #851 April 1998. At the time of writing the paper was available on the site of Professor Richard Wiseman: http://www.richardwiseman.com/resources/ghost-in-machine.pdf

9 – Gilbert White, The Natural History of Selborne, Little Toller Nature Classics 2014, Bat episode p. 48, bold boy episode p.108

10 – 'Awe walks' boost emotional well-being, Medical Xpress 21 Sept 2020.

11 – Dacher Keltner – Awe: The New Science of Everyday Wonder and How It Can Transform Your Life, Penguin Press 2023, quote from p.138

12 – Studs Terkel, Working: People Talk About What They Do All Day and How They Feel About What They Do, Pantheon 1974

13 – University of Manchester, Having a bad job can be worse for your health than being unemployed 11 August 2017. A summary of the study appears on the university's web pages at: https://www.manchester.ac.uk/discover/news/having-a-bad-job/ from where there is a link to the full paper which was published in the Journal of Epidemiology.

14 – Alyson Shontell, A 69-Year-Old Monk Who Scientists Call The 'World's Happiest Man' Says The Secret To Being Happy Takes Just 15 Minutes A Day, The Independent 12 Sept 2020, https://www.independent.co.uk/life-style/69-year-old-monk-who-scientists-call-world-s-happiest-

man-says-secret-being-happy-takes-just-15-minutes-day-a7869166.html

15 - Kurt Vonnegut, Interview promoting "Man Without a Country." Interview conducted by David Brancaccio, NOW (PBS), 7 October 2005


## The War on Mystery


1 – Interview currently online at popaheadwound blogspot:
http://popheadwound.blogspot.com/2008/06/inte rview-war-on-drugs.html

2 – The link posted here was live at the time of writing on the site of Crocus. Other garden centres with and without café facilities are available! https://www.crocus.co.uk/features/ /articleid.988 /

3 – Simon Sinek, Leaders eat Last, Penguin 2014, p.95

4 – Ron Suskind, Faith, Certainty and the Presidency of George W. Bush, New York Times Magazine, Oct. 17, 2004

5 – Christopher Allen's blog post "Life with Alacrity" considers the significance of Dunbar's findings:
http://www.lifewithalacrity.com/2004/03/the_dun bar_numb.html

6 – Laurence Scott, The Four-Dimensional Human: Ways of Being in the Digital World, Heinemann 2015, social media quote (pxix), everywhereness (p.11) ending and not ending (p.116) porn suffix (p. 126-127) encroaching desert (p.224)

7 – Scott, p.211

8 – Paul Lewis, Our minds can be hijacked': the tech insiders who fear a smartphone dystopia, The Guardian 6 Oct 2017, available online as this was written:
https://www.theguardian.com/technology/2017/o ct/05/smartphone-addiction-silicon-valley-dystopia

9 – Center for Humane Technology, https://www.humanetech.com/

10 – BBC News, Nicola Bulley family statement in full, https://www.bbc.co.uk/news/uk-england-lancashire-64707699, 21 February 2023

11 – BBC News, Nicola Bulley: Ex-editor demands scrutiny of media coverage,

https://www.bbc.co.uk/news/uk-england-lancashire-64713045

12 – Timothy E. Moore, Scientific Consensus and Expert Testimony: Lessons from the Judas Priest Trial,  Volume 20, No. 6, November/December 1996, pp 32-38 & 60

13 – This is something you can try for yourself, recordings of some of Deutsch's clips are still available online. http://philomel.com/phantom_words/pages.php?i=1115

14 – Andrew Keen, The Internet is not the Answer, Atlantic Books 2015, the phone/flushing toilet statistic is sourced from a UN report (p. 12), "recursive, circular structure" (p. 57), data factories (p.114),  possible political actions are discussed (pp 231-232)

15 – Sander van der Linden, profile page at University of Cambridge includes click option to coverage of his latest research and media appearances: https://www.psychol.cam.ac.uk/people/sander-van-der-linden

16 – Thoughtful Technology Project, homepage: https://thoughtfultech.org/

17 – Steve Newport, letter to Cumberland and Westmoreland Herald, 19 October 2007: https://www.cwherald.com/a/archive/temple-sowerby-maypole-folklore.298695.html

18 – Neil Nixon, Beatles Myths and Legends, Gonzo Multimedia 2016, pp 69-95

19 – At the time of writing the interview was on the Russian fan-site, Wingspan: http://www.wingspan.ru/bookseng/hisown/hisown02.html

20 – Billy Connolly, An Audience With Billy Connolly, Channel Four Television 1986. The quotes are from different sections of the performance. Full, unofficial, transcript available here: http://www.ibras.dk/comedy/billy_connolly.htm. A comprehensive trawl of many of Connolly's best "liar for a living" stage routines is available in Tall Tales and Wee Stories, Two Roads 2020

## So What

1 – Intelligent Health: http://www.intelligenthealth.co.uk/

2 – Gavin Maxwell, Ring of Bright Water, Little Toller 2014, p.13


3 – "Carlisle produced a performance of the highest quality"                                                   – https://www.youtube.com/watch?v=M2qmzek7uf c

4 – Perhaps, more accurately Franklin popularised a thought that had previously appeared in the The Political History of the Devil (1726) by Daniel Defoe. Defoe may well have taken it from the play The Cobbler of Preston by Christopher Bullock (1716) which includes the line "'Tis impossible to be sure of any thing but Death and Taxes." Technically taxes aren't a certainty. You could escape paying taxes though the circumstances would likely involve continued poor luck in life, a lifestyle choice that flouted legality or put you at the extreme lower end of the income bracket or you could be born to money and live in a tax haven. Death, on the other hand…